BOYCOTT

By

Chinazom Akobundu Godwin

Dedication

For

Engr. Chukwuma S Godwin Agu and
his amiable wife, Mrs. Susan Godwin Agu,
your blessings have yielded fruit.
Thanks a million, times!

ACKNOWLEDGEMENT

A million thanks to Mrs. Gift Foraine Amukoyo and Miss Funmi Akintade for your immeasurable encouragement to complete this novel.

CHAPTER ONE

Gimba stood with bombs laced around his waist in the middle of a crowded Abuja Motor Park. The bombs were covered with agbada so that no one noticed the danger. He flexed an arm as he asked some passersby for directions to get a bus to Gwagwalada. His huge and intimidating demeanor gave him special attention coupled with the *agbada* he had on with beads wound around his arms. His height dissuaded people from seeing the tension on his face. No one would be able to tell he was a suicide bomber.

A young man stopped and pointed in the direction of the motor park. Gimba nodded absentmindedly and walked towards the path without a show of appreciation to his guide. After a few minutes' walk, he stopped, looked to his right, and impatiently walked further to board a bus to Karishi.

It was the period that marked the beginning of harmattan season, which left the Northern soil dry with thunderstruck cracks on the ground. The small river beside the ever-bustling Mararaba bus park had turned dry causing observant passersby to wonder if there was once a river or it had been their imagination.

The North was extreme when it came to weather conditions. When it was rainy, the cold was freezing and when it turned harmattan, the slicing wind was biting, and the scorching sun can cause many people to scuttle for shelter except in places where there were no rooms for succor.

The scorching sun shone mercilessly on the impatient passengers waiting for their tickets. The street hawkers went about selling their wares with no worry as they were used to being under the sun or in the rain; whichever season that met them hustling for daily survival.

Ene, a young and beautiful woman with the body of an international model arrived at the bus park. She scanned the park for any available bus transiting to the main city of Abuja. She needed to meet with the man she had met a week ago at the shopping mall. She could not miss the appointment for anything in the world.

She hastily made her way to a small white sienna bus parked beside several unmoving buses whilst her waist beads and ankle chain jingled in rhythm to her speed. She caught the queasy glances some passengers cast in her direction and held their gaze without batting an eyelash.

"Fine girl see your ticket. Take and bring the money." The Ticket Officer said with a gruff voice.

She gave him a careless grin, flaunting her cleavage while he tore out a ticket for her.

"Have a safe trip." He watched her through a smoldering gaze and licked his lips. "Garki, Wuse." He resumed his chant of attracting potential travelers.

She joined the queue of passengers and put on her earphone. She put on her best flirtatious smile when she saw a handsome man clad in a white *kaftan*, a brown jacket, and a red face cap. The smile slid off the moment she saw the Tasbih in his hand.

The way his fingers moved over the beads made her realize he was saying a prayer. He was entirely different from the men she dated. She tried to assess if he could pass off as an extremist because she was interested in getting him to her bed if he did not fit into that description.

When he stood behind her, his strong cologne wafted into her keen nostrils. She wanted to ask if the fragrance was a perfume she knew. She turned around but quickly noticed his eyes darting sideways. He glanced at his black leather wristwatch as though he was expecting time to still.

She faked a cough to get his attention, but it was obvious he would not have batted an eyelid if she had screamed at the top of her voice. She seductively wriggled her body and became exhausted when he gave her an irritated look.

She climbed into the bus, sat beside the window, and scrolled to her favourite music playlist. She thought if she could not get the man's attention, she would at least block his very existence. She scrolled through the list of songs and clicked on Wizkid's *'Brown Skin Girl.'*

Gimba glanced at his wristwatch for the fifth time. He stared at the driver's empty seat and willed for the driver to take the wheels and begin the journey. He frowned and deep lines appeared on his forehead. He raised his head and saw a man dressed in a white long sleeve shirt and brown trousers. The man clutched a big black Holy Bible to his chest like the only thing his soul craved on earth.

"I am Evangelist Mmadu. I preach within the park and your Chairman usually gives me a ticket for half the price." The man said to the parking attendant.

Gimba maliciously stared at Evangelist Mmadu and wondered how a small man could possess such a loud voice. He brushed the thoughts aside and lowered his gaze to his prayer beads while he took his last prayer. He smiled with the rejuvenating belief that he had a bright future ahead of him. He focused on the steering wheel and moved from one prayer bead to the other. When he saw the ticket officer slam a ticket on the evangelist's palm, he was certain the driver would come onboard in no time. The evangelist got into the bus and sat beside Gimba while the park attendant shut the door.

A few minutes later, the driver, a middle-aged man, collected some few wads of Naira notes from the park attendant; he slid into the front seat and turned on the ignition.

The evangelist smiled as soon as he heard the engine roar to life. "Brethren, let us close our eyes in prayer and commit this journey into God's hands."

Ene scrolled through her phone and tapped on the camera application. She needed to take a selfie to post on her Instagram page. The driver pulled out of the park. Gimba squeezed his eyes shut while his mouth switched recklessly.

The evangelist ended the prayer. He ignored some of the passengers' sly comments and began preaching as tiny beads of sweat formed on his head.

"Many didn't wake up today. But it is the will of God that you are alive to witness this moment. So, honour your creator as you join me in thanksgiving." Evangelist Mmadu began a solemn song of praise.

Gimba opened his eyes and sighed. He stared at his

watch and could not conceal his distaste at the young woman making wanton poses as she took some selfies. His eyes glistened with satisfaction that everyone except him was on their way to unknown destinations. He was not sorry for what he was about to do because he was doing the will of Allah. Evangelist Mmadu was about raising another worship song…

"Allahu Akbar," Gimba exclaimed. There was an explosive sound.

The jarring sound threw the bustling park into pandemonium. The explosion burnt a major section of the park along with countless private cars and commercial vehicles. Some of the hawkers scampered to safety. A great number of people rushed towards the scene, astounded at the level of destruction. A black mass of smoke darkened the once clear sky.

"Call the fire station," someone shouted.

"It is the Danladians again. This was a suicide bombing." Another person screamed.

Tears rolled down the park attendant's face. He could not believe that a passenger he had given a ticket was a suicide bomber. Hoarse voices rend the air until some journalists and police officers came to the scene.

'It is an unforgettable day as the nation witnesses yet

another attack from the Danladians. This ruthless group has struck once more at a public park eliminating scores of innocent people.' The News Anchor's voice reeled from the mic. *'The ruthless group has struck once more....'*

***

The next day, one of the transport owners came to the park. After he assessed the ruin, he shook his head and dabbed his eyes sullen from tears. "Only God will help this country." He gave a ragged sigh and looked across the road.

There was a newspaper stand and people hovered around the vendor. Curious eyes were busy checking the front pages of the newspaper. **Danladians Strike Again…** covered the front pages of the major newspapers.

A group of men argued about politics and moved on to discuss the Danladians. Some men excused themselves from the group because the Danladians were a dreaded name on everyone's lips. The scanty group of commentators expressed their disgust for the country and cursed the Danladians, hoping that they would die or suffer the consequences of their actions through the law.

CHAPTER TWO

Tanko turned off the car stereo, angrily unbuckled his seat belt, and got out of the car. It had barely been twenty-four hours the Danladians struck; he was weary of hearing the same news headlines. He had other pressing matters to attend, which had brought him to the airport's parking area.

Tanko reminiscence relaxing on his king-sized bed and quickly snapped to reality. Such luxury did not hold any importance when he had to welcome the woman that had kept his heart beating beautifully. His heart skipped at an alternating tempo while his palms grew moist. He had not felt like this for anyone except her. His excitement grew each time he caught a glimpse of people pushing their carts towards different vehicles.

He stepped from his Range Rover and scrolled through his iPhone. He looked up when he got close to the arrival's double doors. His eyes darted towards the exit door. He saw his reflection on the windshield of another car. He smiled, knowing his face still held the captivating look that melted hearts. Tanko had wondered if Jumai would still find him attractive. His eyes roamed over his blue-cottoned shirt and black jeans.

"I'm casual enough," Tanko recalled the moment Jumai had told her friend that she liked it when men dressed in a civil style.

Tanko was adjusting the collar of his shirt when two elegantly dressed ladies in trousers, long blouses, and matching scarfs, walked out the exit door in earnest chatter. Tanko was in time to see Fatima Lekwot, and his gaze quickly trailed the woman behind her. His heart fluttered when he saw the feminine figure behind her.

He sighed and thought the woman could be no other than his love, Jumai Biu. He would recognize her even amid multiple women. He strengthened his shoulders and gallantly posed by the sidewalk. "I just need her to walk right into my arms and give me that hug I've been dreaming of."

Tanko was perplexed when he saw Fatima open the back door of a black Sedan and deposit hers and Jumai's luggage in the back seat.

He fumed. "Did she not see me standing feet away? Or was she not told that I was coming to pick them up?" He rubbed his chest, "Calm your heart, Tanko. Perhaps, this is just a misunderstanding. And if it is not, I will just walk up to that Sedan, yank her off the car and warn that Fatima not to drive a wedge between my future bride and me." He nodded, "Yes."

He took a step and realized he was late as the Sedan zoomed out of the parking space. Tanko watched the car drive past, his eyes locked with Jumai's, and she turned to Fatima as if he was invisible. He angrily walked to his car and bowed his head on the steering wheel.

CHAPTER THREE

The President scrutinized the anxious faces around the conference table. "First on today's agenda is the fight against the Danladians and their sponsors." His stare was restive on Alhaji Suleiman before he adjusted his microphone and cleared his throat. "There's a rumour that Danladians plan to bomb the stadium during the football match with England. You all know what that means. Such should not happen on our soil and with the British at that. We must stop this terrorist group with security tact." The president brooded over the sentiments that the terrorist group was out to make his tenure look bloody.

"Yes, Mr. President, we must stop them." Alhaji Biu, the senate majority leader of APP spoke.

The other party members gave a slight nod and whispered amongst themselves.

"Report has it that some policemen spotted some suspected terrorists around the stadium. In the heat of the chase, the criminals abandoned their cars and fled the scene. When the officers searched the vehicle, they found some explosives. This happened two weeks after the bomb blast at the local park. We can't have a repeat." The President beckoned at Alhaji Biu to speak.

Alhaji Biu shook his head. "Your Excellency, I can assure you and the party that a thorough investigation to nab these criminals is on. Give us three months. It's all I ask." He prayed that the pensive look on the president's face was not a reflection of a negative thought to his proposition.

The President tapped his desk for emphasis. "Time is not on our side. The masses want results. If I go down has an incompetent leader, our party, which is the ruling party, will not stand a fairground during the next election. Two weeks is all I give to the resolution of this menace."

Alhaji Biu exhaled and choked on his words to revolt against the little timeframe. He nodded. "Your Excellency. Two weeks is not enough to solve this."

The President nodded and moved closer to the mic. "The second thrust of this meeting is to formally declare my re-election bid." He appraised the expressions on the party members' faces and smiled over the welcoming glances that greeted his announcement until he saw the scowl on Alhaji Suleiman's face.

"I can even decide to run for the third term in office, and there is nothing anybody can do." The President added.

His last statement threw the tranquil conference room into chaos. Alhaji Suleiman and some governors began to murmur in disapproval.

"Why would he run for the second term?" A Northern governor yelled.

A Southern governor turned on him with fury in his eyes. "Why won't he run for a second term? It is people like you that cause segregation in politics."

Alhaji Biu glanced at his friend, Alhaji Taminu, and waved his arms in helplessness. Alhaji Taminu shook his head and came in-between the irked governors.

It exasperated Alhaji Biu to see these grownups act like toddlers. "It's enough." His gruff voice boomed across the hall.

It took some moments for the party members' murmur to fade and grave silence enveloped the hall.

"We are the leaders; we are the kingmakers, why are we propagating disparity due to individual interests?" Alhaji Biu said in a hoarse tone.

Alhaji Suleiman stood and held on tight to his flowing *agbada*. He had thought the president was joking about his re-election bid when he had told him about it a year ago, but the president's formal announcement stirred an unpleasant feeling. He did not care if his veins popped out in anger in the full glare of other members. "Your excellency, you had promised and signed with the party to run a single tenure."

The President scoffed. Alhaji Suleiman was a fool to think he would rule for a term. Power had intoxicated him, and he would do anything to hold on to this sweet power. "And what is the big deal if I decide to run for one more tenure like my predecessors?"

"Mr President, I, Alhaji Suleiman Dantata will not allow that, *wallahi*. No way," He beat his chest. "I am from the northern majority and I agreed to run as vice president with you because we agreed that you would let me have the presidential ticket after your first tenure."

Although he could remember when he had had the deal with his then running mate, the President shrugged and pretended to go through some papers on his desk. "I can't remember having such bargain with you, Alhaji Suleiman Dantata."

Alhaji Suleiman vehemently stared at the President. "Deny it all you want, Mr. President. I promise you, I will not sit back and let that happen, never."

To offset the rising chaos in the conference room, Alhaji Taminu, the APP party's chairman stood and flagged his arms for decorum to return to normalcy. "Please, stop this before our opponents use this against us. We shouldn't forget that walls have ears. "Haba, Alhaji Sule, we expect much from you. You are the vice president."

"It is best if you remind him. I will not tolerate such insubordination." The President stood. "I am no longer comfortable with this man. I will make sure to see to the needful."

Alhaji Suleiman yelled and banged the table. "That's a lie, Mr. President. You are the president because of me." He jabbed his chest with a finger. "The people supported you because of me. Look, Mr. President, you just shot yourself in the foot. With this move, you will not have it rosy with your reign."

The governors and other party members began to argue amongst themselves. Alhaji Biu gently placed a hand on the President's hand to stop him from speaking.

The President grinned. "You see. He has confessed." He pointed at Alhaji Suleiman. "This man is behind all the bombings and all the unscrupulous elements terrorizing this country to tarnish my image before the people of this country and the international community. He must be arrested."

Alhaji Biu worriedly looked around the growing violent scene. "Please, everyone should calm down. Please, may we all sit?"

Alhaji Biu waited for everyone to sit before he spoke. "It's so disheartening to see us fight ourselves over tomorrow that is yet to come. If it pleases Allah, we may not even live to see it." He ignored their unsatisfied stare questioning and rebutting his stance on life and death. "Yes, it's the truth. From our individual faith, we know that our tomorrow is not certain. So why are we fighting? Let us concentrate on the unity of our party and the betterment of our country."

Alhaji Taminu nodded with a satisfied smile in his eyes. He began clapping. "Well done, Alhaji Bui. Well said."

Other party members joined in the applause. Alhaji Suleiman found the statement uninteresting and stood abruptly. "No amount of money can save you this time, Mr. President. If you like, squander the entire budget on your political jingoism. I, Alhaji Suleiman Dantata will not be a party to your jiggery-pokery and malicious tactics."

The President waved him off. "We shall see about that, Vice President Suleiman."

Alhaji Suleiman scoffed. "So be it." He gave disgusting look to the President, picked up his phones, and walked away amid voices calling him to halt.

The meeting ended after the party members

observed all formal protocols. Alhaji Biu and other politicians stepped out of the hall discussing in different groups and the press advanced on them.

A young male reporter focused his recorder on Alhaji Biu as he towered over the throng of journalists to interview the senate majority leader. "Sir, in a fit of rage, Alhaji Suleiman has disclosed that the president has breached a personal oath in his bid to return for a second term. What do you have to say about this development that can shatter your party before the next general elections?"

Alhaji Biu hesitated for a few seconds and cleared his throat. He wondered how the walls got hold of this information. He could not reckon the ghostly excesses of the media.

"Sir," another reporter said impatiently. "Is your party strong enough to handle the brewing storm?"

Alhaji Biu nodded and confidently smiled into the cameras. "Yes. Mr. President has declared his interest to run for a second tenure. As a party, we owe him the duty to support and guide him through good governance."

A female reporter's voluminous breasts thrust to Alhaji Biu before her phone reached his lips. "Is it true that the President is breaching the contracts he signed with the party? Is it true he vowed to run a single term and now planning to continue in governance?"

Alhaji Biu gave her a warm smile and jammed his hands in the folds of his *agbada*. If he were not feeling strained from the political party's crisis, he would have devised a way to charm and welcome her with all pleasure at one of his guesthouses. "I don't think I'm in the right position to answer that question. If Mr. President wants to embark on a race to another term, then so be it." He spoke.

The reporter stared at Alhaji Biu's lips and let her gaze trail to his heart as if she could weave a magic wand to make him speak in all honesty. She was more disappointed when Alhaji Biu arrogantly waved off her and her colleagues and walked away.

Alhaji Biu and some party members walked towards the parking area amidst some hearty conversations. Each man shook hands and bowed at the other as they got into their respective cars.

Deep thought of going home to rest without any interruption beset Alhaji Biu's mind as he signaled to his driver. "Take me home."

The driver ran in haste to open the door to the back seat and drove off the moment Alhaji Biu relaxed.

CHAPTER FOUR

The birds' chirps atop a mango tree excited Yusuf. He moved a black Bishop piece to block the white King already held in check by a black Pawn and Rook. His grin widened. The fact that he was about to win in the game of chess doubled his excitement.

"Checkmate," Yusuf threw his head backward in victorious laughter and rested his back against the tree.

Garuba threw away his chewing stick and waved his hands in dismissal of the game. He was angry and disappointed at himself for losing another game to Yusuf. The audience clapped to Yusuf's victory. Some laughed as Garuba's face grew sullen with anger and Yusuf joined them.

"What do you people know about chess? Will you stop clapping into my ears? It's irritating!" Garuba said in Hausa.

Yusuf stopped laughing. He wondered why his friend took their little fun to heart. "Relax, Garuba. It's just a game."

"It is a sour game because I'm yet to have a win." He hissed. There had to be something about chess that his friend kept secret from him, otherwise, a game of chess should be a game of victory like other games they played.

Yusuf tilted an eyebrow and winked at Garuba. "I will always be the master." He beat his chest and chuckled.

Garuba's anger vanished as if it never crossed his face. There was no way he could stay mad at his friend for a long time. He pointed at him. "I have a feeling you are not playing a fair game." He stamped a foot on the ground and gave Yusuf a quizzical look. "One day, I shall catch up with your tricks or fair skills."

Yusuf's jaw dropped. "Are you serious?" Garuba's unsmiling face told him he meant every word. "Come on, Garuba, accept defeat, and have a reason to fight again. So, what do you say about another game?" He smirked.

Garuba thought he had another chance to become a winner. He took a fresh chewing stick and jammed it in-between his teeth. "Why not, mate? Today seems quite cool to play countless games." He clasped his hands, "Let's bring it on."

Yusuf inhaled the fresh atmosphere with his eyes closed and thought the serenity was the one reason he would prefer to live all his life in the village than the noisy and polluted city. The village had fewer irritants and nothing could compare to the clean air the villagers breathe. They would not exchange it for basic social amenities and industrialization. He opened his eyes and sighed. "Let the game begin." He arranged the chess pieces.

Garuba's gaze wandered towards the arranged pieces and he grew meditative as different thoughts assailed his mind. "I've been thinking."

"Of what, mate. You think because you are. Is that not why you are human with a thinking faculty?" Yusuf laughed and righted a falling pawn.

"Stop fooling around. Yusuf, I mean what I said."

Yusuf chuckled aloud. "But my dear friend, you're yet to say anything."

Yusuf set the game and looked up to Garuba who looked rather lost in whatever world he had built in his mind.

"Garuba, what's wrong? I've not seen you this worried in a long while."

Garuba's tone was sober with uncertainty. "I've been thinking seriously about the Danladians."

Yusuf's face contorted into a dark grimace. "What about the Danladians? I thought we'd been through that discussion. Garuba, you must stay away. Those guys are not good." Yusuf desperately needed to convince his friend against dreaming of an association with the Danladians. "Look, mate, I…"

"Yusuf, you have to understand…"

"Should I understand that you're having considerations to become a paid killer fighting the government? Murdering people?" He did not care if he was raising his voice for the world to hear. If that would cause his friend to get his head right, then he would yell until his voice grew hoarse. After all, the power of crime is in its secrecy.

"They kill the infidels and the oppressive government."

"This is unbelievable. Where are these foolish words coming from? Have you forgotten so soon the words of Imam Mukhtar, Allah bless his soul, concerning these people? He calls them the real infidels. Garuba, tell me the truth. Swear. Who have you been talking to?"

Yusuf was about to say something else when they heard sporadic gunshots from nearby. His heart raced. Yusuf turned in the direction of the gunshots in fear. The young adults laid down flat and hid their faces in the dust. He could hear their whimper and call to mercy from Allah to save them. Yusuf cursed, wishing there was something he could do to save the people or better still, save the village from these infidels.

The gunshots increased and some people scuttle to

escape. Suddenly, the trucks approached, and some people had already wet their pants from hearing screechy wheels. The members of the group jumped down from the trucks like birds. Garuba peeked through his fingers and glimpsed the leader of the dreaded group with a cigar in hand.

Garuba swallowed the moment he realized that the leader, Inuwa Isa was a huge dark man with an ugly face riddled with scars. Inuwa's scars made his inside crawl with fear. He cringed and wished the ground would suddenly open and swallow him when Inuwa began to walk towards them.

Inuwa kicked off the chessboard with his huge black boot. Yusuf and Garuba shivered and hid their faces in the dust. He eyed them and kicked each of them on their buttocks. "Your mates are out there fighting the true cause and pleasing Allah with their lives. You morons are here playing chess." He spat and glanced at the other people who had also lain on the floor out of fear. "If you seek a better life; we are ready to give you ₦5 million."

The huge amount got the attention of some boys. Inuwa barked out laughter, and the mockery was not lost on the boys who had stopped whimpering to hear more of what the leader of the Danladians had to say.

Satisfied that he got their attention, Inuwa smirked and

continued, "Join the fight and your family gets ₦5 Million and you get ten virgins from Allah." He grinned, imagining what it would be like to enjoy ten beautiful virgins in peace, away from all the ruffles of the world. He took a few steps towards Yusuf.

Inuwa dragged Yusuf up and tipped his face upwards to face him. "You, what is your name?" He studied his smooth face with a stubborn chin. Inuwa smiled and thought the boy was the recruit the Danladians wanted in their cause.

He set his stubborn chin. "Yusuf Ibrahim."

"Yusuf Ibrahim, do you believe in Allah?" Inuwa asked.

Yusuf silently cursed at the ridiculous question. The village was practically a Muslim community so what else would he believe in if not in Allah? He stomached his disdain instead. "I do, I believe in Allah."

"So why are you not fighting for him? You are supposed to be in the war front and slaughter many for Allah." His angry breath fanned Yusuf's face.

Yusuf could not reveal he was vulnerable as the others. "I don't think Allah would want me to kill the innocent."

Another soldier who was just about Inuwa's body frame smacked him on the face and flung a swearword at him. Yusuf eyed him and spat out blood on the ground.

Inuwa fumed in anger. He dragged him up and pushed

him against the huge tree. "Are you saying we are stupid for fighting Allah's battle?"

Yusuf gasped for breath. Inuwa released his hold on him, and he spat blood again on the ground. He braced to speak with bloodied tongue. "I just can't see the sense in killing helpless people. My Quran is against taking the lives of the innocent, and Allah would not want me to trade my life for Five Million Naira."

The soldier smacked Yusuf again and aimed his rifle at him.

Yusuf drooled in fear. He thought if Inuwa gave the soldier a command to shoot, then he would be dead meat.

Inuwa tightened his hold on Yusuf and grinned evilly when Yusuf groaned. He could choke the life out of Yusuf that instant because he was angry, he dared to talk back at him. "Are you now saying that your life is better than those who joined the cause?"

Yusuf winced. "I cannot sell my life for Five Million Naira."

Inuwa dragged Yusuf off the tree, pushed him to the ground, and set his rifle ready for the kill. But a lanky Danladian soldier rushed towards him and whispered into his ears.

Inuwa groaned on hearing that the Nigerian soldiers

were coming towards the village. He turned to Yusuf, "Today is your lucky day." He turned around and marched into the truck with the others matching his strides. Within minutes, the trucks retreated into the forest.

The other men got off the ground and scampered into their houses. Garuba stood and helped Yusuf to sit on the bench.

"Why are you always found in the tent of stubbornness?" He gave Yusuf a curious grin while observing the deep cut on his bloodied mouth.

Yusuf picked up his chessboard, stashed it into the chess box, and walked away. He had little remarks to spare on some notorious terrorist group or about how close he came to losing his life.

CHAPTER FIVE

Asokoro was the home of high socialites in Abuja. Alhaji Biu's neighbour was the former ambassador to France. Aside from the fact that the estate housed the high socialites of Abuja, he also liked the peace and tranquility of the estate.

"Alhaji, we're here." The driver announced.

Alhaji Biu sighed with contentment the moment his driver drove into his gigantic residence. One of his bodyguards opened the car door for him. He gathered his flowing outfit and slid out of the car. He took a satisfying look at the well-clipped lawn around the water fountain planted in the middle of the compound. The well-trimmed purple hibiscus was a remarkable sight. He caught a glimpse of some female servants trooping in and out of the house. He marched into the house in long strides.

His bodyguards stood outside while he strode into the exquisitely furnished mansion with twelve bedrooms. He was proud of his achievements. Owning a house in an expensive estate in the most expensive suburb of Abuja was an envy to some of his colleagues.

He remembered how he had bought the house from his first allowance when he became a senator several years ago. That was before he met others who turned his life around by introducing him to the better part of politics that involved making money, being in power, and never really getting involved in the process.

Alhaji Biu shook his head, "Politics is indeed a dirty game that only the brave could make some clean money."

"Baba," Jumai screamed.

Alhaji Biu beamed when he saw his daughter climb down the stairs. Jumai was his heartbeat, his treasure and he did not mind buying the whole world for her. She had grown more beautiful just like her mother. It was until she drew closer that he realized how much he had missed his only child. "Ah, my delightful daughter, you're home."

Jumai bobbed. "Yes, Baba. I missed you so much."

He engulfed her in a warm embrace. "Welcome home, my daughter. How was your trip?"

Jumai pulled out of his arms and flashed a complacent smile. "Everything went smoothly baba. It is good to be home again."

He looked up just in time to see his daughter's friend. "Fatima, how are you?"

"I am fine, Alhaji." Fatima Lekwot bowed in greeting. "Baba, you're looking good. You've added weight from the last time I saw you."

Alhaji Biu laughed fondly. "All praises be to Allah and Jumai's mother."

Fatima smiled, "You're right, Baba."

"Long time no see. How is your father?" He moved to sit on one of the sofas when his friend walked in. Jumai and Fatima greeted Alhaji Taminu, but he waved in response as he was on a phone call.

"My father is fine. I told him I would stop by at your home. He sent his regards." Fatima clasped her hands.

"Tell him I don't want his regards. I need his support, he will understand." Alhaji Biu summoned a maid to pour him a drink. He needed a strong drink to shake off the stunt the President had pulled off at the conference.

"I shall tell him, Alhaji." Fatima smiled demurely.

Alhaji Biu looked to Jumai, "My dearest, daughter. I would've come to pick you up at the airport despite my busy schedule but Tanko had insisted he would do that. I'm sure he gave you girls a leisurely ride." He grinned, savouring the thought of being young and in love again. He stopped his thoughts abruptly. "Wait, where is he?"

A light frown grazed Jumai's face as she moved towards

the stairs. One more talk about Tanko would get her tearing the whole house down. "I don't know, Baba." She gritted her teeth. "Am I his keeper? Why should I know his whereabouts?"

Alhaji Biu smiled curiously. "What did you say?"

Jumai fiddled with her headgear. "No, it's nothing, Baba."

"Come here, have you greeted my friend?" He gestured to Alhaji Taminu who had ended his telephone conversation and silently walked in on them.

Jumai forced a smile and approached Alhaji Taminu. She ignored his wide grin and bobbed. She knew what men like them wanted and she hated it.

"Our wife, how are you?" Alhaji Taminu asked.

Jumai hesitated. "I'm fine, Alhaji." She said softly.

Alhaji Taminu noticed the lingering frown on Jumai's face.

"That is good. It is well that you are back. I'm sure you must have been missing my Tanko too." Alhaji Taminu turned to his friend who was grinning recklessly. "I know that look. We will formally make our intentions known, soon."

Jumai ignored him and stood. She was not eager to ruin her beautiful day by getting angry. "I have to go. Please, extend my greetings to your family."

Alhaji Taminu smiled, "I'm eager to deliver your greetings to them."

"Baba, how's mom? I've not heard her voice since we arrived."

"I'm sure she's somewhere in the house." Alhaji Biu turned on his phone.

Jumai hugged her father before ascending the stairs in search of her mother. Fatima followed closely behind.

Alhaji Taminu got lost in Fatima's curves accentuated by her jeans trousers. He stared at her swaying buttocks until she was out of sight. Her light-skinned face fascinated him more than her sexy body.

Alhaji Taminu laughed. "Allah, if you didn't shoot down the idea, I swear I would have made her mine." He sighed. The image of Fatima Lekwot's swinging buttocks flashed in his mind. He became sober thinking he would never get such pleasure.

"My friend, you had better concentrate. We have pressing matters to attend." Alhaji Biu chuckled loudly.

Alhaji Taminu sighed in defeat and sat next to his friend.

CHAPTER SIX

After the Danladians struck, the villagers seldom went to their farms because some farmers had died on that fateful day, and others were missing. The situation had driven Yusuf berserk, and it was painful he could not bring much succor to the bereaved.

After days of mourning and searching for the missing farmers, he relaxed to take care of his sick father who was near the point of death. Yusuf returned home early from the farm and found the herbalist tending his father. He became scared when he saw some members of his family squatted on the other side of his father's mat while his mother wept uncontrollably at a corner of the hut.

Yusuf rushed inside and squatted beside the herbalist. His father coughed loudly and winced. He slowly opened his eyes and the weary eyeballs danced of pains. He had another wracking cough and closed his eyes.

"*Sai* Baba, please find healing through this medication." Yusuf glanced at his father's frail body and shook his head.

"This is getting serious. We need to get *sintua* leaf immediately." The herbalist adjusted the cow-skin bag slung across his neck. He sat on the mat and faced Yusuf's father who was still coughing.

Yusuf's mother wiped the tears with the back of her hand as hope shone in her dark eyes. She may look tall and strong on the outside, but she was weak and small inside. She could not bear to lose her husband. "How do we get it?" She sat up.

The herbalist looked in the direction of the setting sun. "In the next village of Zaka, we'll need ₦6, 000."

Yusuf bowed at the herbalist, nodded at his mother, and exited the hut in a hurry. His mother followed him. She led Yusuf to the back of the hut.

Tears rolled down her face as she stared at her son. "Yusuf, there is no kobo left in this house. How can we get ₦6,000 to save your father? I had used the last money I had to prepare breakfast for Jumai, your daughter. I don't know what she will eat by nightfall. We were near starvation. Do something very fast!"

Yusuf sighed and squeezed his mother's shoulder. "Don't worry, mother. We'll have something to eat and keep us alive." He turned around, stood for a while, and walked away. He thought of how his brave words to his mother would come to fruition.

Yusuf was at crossroads, unsure of how to raise that

amount of money in a short time. He was about to take the route to the market when he remembered his friends, Ahmed, and Sakha. He took the left turn that led to their house. He hoped and prayed to get a positive response from them.

Ahmed was stepping out of their newly built bungalow when he met Yusuf. He smoothed the ruffles on his brown *kaftan* and smiled as Yusuf approached him. They shook hands and Ahmed noticed Yusuf's grip was unusually weak.

Ahmed noted Yusuf's distraught countenance. "You don't look well. What's the matter?"

"I," Yusuf hesitated.

"Please, my friend. Tell me what's happening. You don't look happy. What is this sadness written all over you? I hope all is well at home?"

Yusuf sighed and told Ahmed what the problem was while his eyes roamed over the modernly built house. He wondered when his friend erected a proper building instead of the thatched hut their father had built.

"Please, you have to help me. Ahmed, my father is dying." His voice trembled.

Ahmed shook his head. "Kai, Yusuf. I have told you before. I don't have money of my own. The little one I have is for our family's business." He flung a hand towards the house. "Sakha signed up with the Danladians so that we can have a better life."

Yusuf moved backward in shock. How could Sakha sign up with the Danladians because of Five Million Naira? "Please, Ahmed. I'm going to pay back." He bent his head backward to stop the tears threatening to run down his cheeks.

Ahmed touched his shoulder. "I'm sorry, Yusuf. There's nothing I can do." He stepped away from Yusuf. "If you will excuse me, I have pressing matters to deal with." He winked. "I've got a date with the girl I want to marry."

Yusuf moved out of his way and Ahmed proudly opened the car door and got in. Seeing Yusuf in this pathetic situation made him realize his fortune of having a devoted brother who was ready to kill in exchange for a better life for his family. He was happy his brother was not like Yusuf who claimed that the Danladians were not doing the will of Allah. He gave a derisive laugh and muttered. "Poverty would surely end the likes of Yusuf. I'm sure of that."

Yusuf watched him drive off. He turned and left the compound. On his way home, he met Sanni, his friend's younger brother. He was clad in the same attire as Ahmed with a different colour. He stopped and told Sanni about his predicament.

Sanni was sober at first but then he remembered how his brother had given them a better life in exchange for his own. He shook his head and gave Yusuf a taunting smile. "Yusuf, I feel your plight. But I'm sorry, I can't help you."

"Sanni, I beg you in the name of Allah. I am going to pay back." He clasped his hands in a plea.

Sanni raised a hand. "Yusuf, please, I'm not in the mood for nonsense. If you want a better life for your family, join the Danladians like my brother, Ganni did. He gave his life so I can take care of my parents. Goodbye."

Yusuf felt all hope was lost as he watched Sanni walk away.

Yusuf returned home in time to see his father slip into unconsciousness. From the entrance of the hut, he watched the herbalist try to resuscitate him, but his father was unmoving. He dashed into the house on hearing his mother's wails. He dropped to his knees in agony as tears rolled down his cheeks.

Yusuf let out a piercing cry, "No, Baba." He angrily beat his chest. "If I was man enough, I would have been able to save my father. He would still be breathing. Oh, Allah. What kind of a cursed son am I?"

Yusuf slowly rose from the floor and cleaned his tears.

He walked out of the house while his daughter, Jumai ran into his arms. She held unto her father as tears rolled down her flaccid cheeks.

Yusuf held her tightly. "Don't cry, my child. I can't bear to see your tears."

Jumai hiccupped and coughed. She had several dry coughs which caught the attention of almost everyone in the hut.

Yusuf, the herbalist, and Zahra all shared a knowing look and turned to Jumai. Yusuf's heart skipped. His daughter's persistent dry coughs were exactly how his father's illness began until it led to his death. He wobbled towards a bench and sat.

Jumai came to sit by him, and he embraced her in a tight hug. The fear he might lose his daughter weighed heavily in his heart. He loosened his hold and Jumai and stood. He walked towards his hut as he tried to suppress the cry that lodged deep down his throat.

"Am I also going to die like Baba?"

Jumai's quivering voice made him standstill.

Yusuf shuddered and turned to face her. She ran into his opened arms. He could see the fear lurking in her small black eyes. He squatted to her height and held her hands. "Don't say that Jumai, you're not going to die. I won't let anything happen to you." He forced a confident smile in case his voice had betrayed him.

Jumai knew whenever her father was telling a lie. She could tell he was uncertain and scared about her health. She wished she could help him get rid of the fear and grieve over his father's death. She wanted to be strong for her father. Instead, she blurted. "I am scared, Baba. I don't want to die." She burst into tears.

"You will not die, Jumai. I will do everything to make sure you get proper treatment from the hospital." He confidently said.

The next day, Yusuf and some neighbours conducted his father's burial rites. He could not sleep at night. He looked at the roof and thought of ways to save his daughter from dying. Jumai began to cough, and he went over to stay with her in his mother's hut.

Two days later, the village was unusually quiet. The birds chirped happily, singing from tree to tree and perching on thatched rooftops.

Yusuf stepped out of the hut. His daughter had coughed all through the night and it had been difficult to ignore seeing that he sat with her. He had resolved to go miles to save his daughter's life. He would not sit around like a lost toddler when his daughter's life was being threatened. He stepped out of the compound and onto the road that led him to the market in search of a Good Samaritan.

❋ ❋ ❋

Garuba clung tightly to a moving truck. His heart skipped each time they moved farther from his small community. The chants of the other men on the truck made him more aware of his new oath, his new allegiance, and his new responsibility. Even though his friend, Yusuf would have considered him a fool for doing what he did, he felt more like a hero laying his life on the line for his family.

Garuba watched as dust sprung in response to the moving truck as it took a sharp turn on a deserted road. He was not sure what would become of his life now that he had taken the most dreaded decision in his family's history. He wondered if his life would turn out like those suicide bombers he had heard about on the radio. He shrugged over the thought that, that should not be part of his worries since the suicide bombers would be in paradise enjoying their virgins.

The truck suddenly jerked back and forth. Garuba heard the front door open and then close with a bang. When the men went silent, he realized that Inuwa had come down from the truck. No one wanted to bear the brunt of Inuwa's anger because the last man that made that mistake paid the price with his head.

Garuba stared at Inuwa when he heard his dry laugh. Everyone in the truck directed their gaze to Inuwa who was speaking to another man behind the truck. Garuba thought that the Danladians had caught another prey but then, when he caught sight of the familiar jeans and brown T-shirt, his heart skipped. It was Yusuf. He never wanted his friend to see him this way, but he had to act fast.

He jumped out of the truck to save Yusuf. He was afraid that his friend's feisty tongue could cause his end on this dusty road.

"Maybe you're not so lucky today after all." Inuwa smiled slyly and appraised Yusuf with an aura of distinct admiration. He caressed his gun and snorted.

Garuba panicked. He rushed towards Inuwa and bowed his head. "Please, I beg your pardon. He is my good friend. Let me talk some sense into him."

Inuwa nodded and smirked at Yusuf before going to the side of the truck and lit a wrap of marijuana. He smoked and exhaled fat rings of fumes without taking his eyes off Garuba and Yusuf.

Garuba took long strides towards his friend who looked distraught and somewhat frustrated. He wanted to ask if he was all right but the glare on Yusuf's face stopped the words.

"Garuba, why?" Yusuf should be scared for his life or begged to have some money to save Jumai's life but instead, he found himself being a concerned friend.

Garuba looked exasperated. "Yusuf, it's not my fault. I mean, think about it. How long are we to remain *talakawas?* I want the good life too for my wife and children. Is it bad to wish the best for them? The best I cannot have. The best I can give them?"

Yusuf scoffed and sadly shook his head. "You're making it sound like these guys are going to give you a job in an office. Garuba, in case you've forgotten, their operations involve killing people."

"Lower your voice, Yusuf. They could hear us."

Yusuf did not care if he sounded like a killjoy or if Inuwa could hear his voice. All he wanted was for his friend to get back on the good track.

Garuba was close to shedding tears. "No. They kill those that support this useless government that has done nothing for you and me."

Garuba remembered how the whole village had suffered for more than ten years before the local government repaired the only borehole in the community. The community's clinic was ill-equipped and there were no schools for children. He had lost hope in the irresponsible government. Garuba avoided Yusuf's questioning look and shifted his gaze to the only tree that stood at the roadside. He felt rage whenever the government kept diverting funds meant for developing the community into their pockets.

Yusuf sighed. "Garuba, the government may have its lapses, but I don't think that's enough reason for us to start killing innocent people who are trying very hard to succeed just like you and I. Allah never recommended that."

Garuba appeared lost in thought and Yusuf touched his shoulder to get his attention. Garuba shrugged Yusuf's hand off his shoulder and took some steps backward.

Yusuf sadly looked at the truck. "Garuba, please, this is a mistake. You'll be committing a big sin. Allah will administer justice to offenders of his teachings. Leave justice to Allah."

Garuba shook his head. "Yusuf, the problem is not a problem until a problem becomes your problem. When you are finally in my shoes, you will understand that every action whether right or wrong has a driving force."

Inuwa smoked the second wrap of marijuana and turned towards Garuba. He called out to him, "Hey, Garuba. It's time to go. We need to get to camp as quickly as possible since the day is still young, and the camp is far from the village."

Garuba bowed towards Inuwa. He turned to Yusuf and spoke hastily. "I have to give it a try. I will probably see you in the afterlife, my friend." He nodded to reassure himself of the commitment to die serving the cause. He nodded again and walked away.

Yusuf hopelessly raised his arms and let it fall by his sides in defeat. "What about your wife and children?"

Garuba turned around and spoke in a faint voice. "I will have a chance to make their life better without me." He turned away and wiped the tears rolling down his cheeks. He smiled weakly and climbed into the truck.

Inuwa seized up Yusuf. "Go home and play chess, boy. Let men do Allah's business." He barked a burst of sinister laughter and spat close to Yusuf's feet before he got into the truck.

Inuwa slammed the door of the passenger's seat and the driver started the truck. "Circle the truck around that hopeless fool," Inuwa commanded the driver to drive around Yusuf and ordered his men to shoot sporadically into the air.

Yusuf cowered in fear and fell to the ground when he heard the gunshots. He thought that his time was over and that his daughter would meet him in the afterlife, but it was not until the trucks stopped swirling around him that he realized that he was still alive.

Relief flooded Garuba's heart the moment he noticed that his friend was alive. The men around him began to chant warfare songs in Hausa, and the realization of who he had become suddenly dawned on him. He looked at the deserted road and wished he could join his friend on the ground, but there was no going back. He waved at the disappearing figure of Yusuf and slowly sank to the floor of the truck. He imagined Yusuf waving him and smiling as he let the tears freely flow down his cheeks.

CHAPTER SEVEN

The stars hid their sparkles behind the moon tonight. Yusuf sat outside and admired the sky. He had come out of the hut because he could not bear to see his daughter in her condition. He felt miserable for not being able to get money for her treatment. He suddenly stood and dashed into the house. He angrily paced around, obviously worried about his life, family, including the unscrupulous government.

He rolled out his sleeping mat and laid on it. His pathetic situation was a hard reality to reckon with whenever the sun came up and went down. He slowly twitched his feet which ached from his fruitless search of money. If only there was a way money could grow on trees, how fortunate it would turn out for him because the cashew and guava trees at his backyard would have been filled with money. At least, the trees were the only natural resource that Allah had blessed them with.

It was quite unfortunate that Allah had not blessed them with money. He sighed and tossed on the mat. Jumai's cough disrupted his thought. He froze on the spot until he could no longer hear her cough. Tears burned the back of his eyes. He could not bear to watch his daughter die. His daughter was a bright girl. There was no way he could allow his future to be laid to rest because he could not fulfill his fatherly duties.

Tears rolled down his cheeks as his mind drifted into the conversation he once had with his daughter. He asked her about what she wanted to become. He recalled that they were seated in front of the house playing his favourite game of chess.

"Why do you love to play chess?" She folded her thin arms.

Jumai was so inquisitive and asked questions per second.

Yusuf smiled excitedly. "It is because it trains the brain to be smart." He moved a black pawn and looked up at Jumai.

She frowned. How does the most complicated game she had ever seen cause the brain to be smart? "How is that possible?" She pointed to her head. "The brain is up here, and the chess is right here." She placed a finger on the chessboard.

Yusuf grinned. "Playing chess helps unleash your

originality, it activates the right side of your brain which is responsible for creativity. It increases problem-solving skills." He sighed softly and playfully held Jumai's cheek. "It enables you to think fast, my dear." He chuckled and dropped his hand.

"Really," her eyes widened with deep interest. "When I grow up, I want to be the smartest scientist in the universe." She beat her chest. She silently thought she wanted to make her Baba proud. and she did not mind becoming a scientist so she could take care of him in the future.

He stared at her quizzically. "Why?"

She sighed and shook her head. Did her Baba not know that their village needed a scientist? "Baba, don't you know that a scientist would care for the community enough to find the solution to any problem." She nodded and said aloud. "Yes, Baba. I want to be a Scientist because I want to find the solution to all the diseases that have been killing people in this community." Her face lightened up with pride.

Yusuf intently stared at Jumai. "And I will make sure your dream comes true."

Jumai's cough shot him out of his reverie. He swallowed hard as he tried to search the dark for answers. The evening breeze was not discreet as it conveyed his mother's silent whimper from the hut where she sat with Jumai. Yusuf mistakenly chewed on his lip and tasted blood. He could feel the darkness in the hut closing in on him, and kind of strangling his throat.

The whole scenario reminded him of Inuwa when he had seen him that morning. He tried so hard to block off Inuwa's voice from coming back to his head but somehow, Inuwa's voice and last statement kept ringing in his head. *'Join the fight and your family gets ₦5 Million, and you get ten virgins from Allah.'*

Jumai coughed violently. Yusuf broke out of his brown study. He wiped his tears and rose to his feet, reluctant to set eyes upon the degenerating condition of his daughter. Just as he was thinking about her persistent cough, Zahra walked into his hut with a lantern.

"How is her condition, Mama?"

She adjusted her headscarf which was almost slipping off. "It's getting worse." Her voice trembled.

Yusuf groaned and buried his face in his palms.

Zahra raised the lantern to her face so she could see her son and he could see how angry she was at him. "I can't lose her." Her eyes were sullen from crying and her voice had become hoarse. "We just buried your father three days ago. Your father died because we could not afford proper medical care. Your father sold everything just to see you through school now he's dead. You could not save him, and you're going to sit here and watch your daughter die too?"

He groaned from frustration and looked up at her. "What would you have me do, Mama?"

"Everything, Yusuf." Tears rolled down her cheeks. "Do anything to save your child. You can ask, borrow, beg, and steal. Do anything, just look for money and save your child."

He wailed. He could not believe his mother would throw such terrible statements at him. Yusuf screamed. "You think I haven't done everything possible to get money. The only option left is to join the Danladians and shed innocent blood. Mama is that what you would have me do?"

Zahra squatted to the floor and wept. She hated their living condition. She wished that life treated her more fairly.

Yusuf lowered his voice. "And that I can never do, Mama. It is not right. It does not please Allah and my soul. So even if I must die, I will never do it."

Jumai walked into the hut. The light from the lantern was enough to reveal to Yusuf that his daughter had heard him. Her face glistened with tears as she rushed into his arms crying. Yusuf clenched his teeth to stop himself from crying. But father and daughter hugged tightly and cried in each other's arms.

In the middle of the night, Yusuf woke and came to check up on his mother and daughter in their hut. He felt relieved when he saw they were fast asleep. He paced around the room in deep thoughts. He stopped moving when Jumai turned and tossed on the mat while coughing. Yusuf prayed his daughter should remain asleep until he had embarked on the task that had set his mind on a new quest in life.

Jumai yawned and stilled to a peaceful slumber. Yusuf picked up his chessboard and arranged the pieces in a small bag. He stared at the chessboard with a nostalgic grin. He had conquered every single person he played chess with, but he wished the disease-fighting his daughter was a game of chess. He would have fought it relentlessly until he won.

He wiped off the tear slipping down his cheek. He shook his head and flexed his shoulder. Now was not the time to cry. It was the time to be audacious. He glanced at his only family with love and stepped into dawn still cloaked by darkness. He took a moment to enjoy the melodious chirping of the birds before he took a lonely path that led to the forest.

CHAPTER EIGHT

Tanko ignored the ESPN channel; there were better things that occupied his mind than European sports analysis blaring from the television.

Jumai had taken over his mind and he needed an explanation on why he would be treated as an unimportant person by his wife-to-be. Did Jumai not know that he was going to be her husband in a few months? He scoffed. If she did not know then he needed to sink it deep into her head soon and he did not care whichever method would make that possible.

The coolness of the room did not excite him, and he did not find pleasure in admiring the exquisite décor like he usually did. He glanced at the brown leather couches and realized that they were different from the set of couches that had complimented the sitting room's ambiance a few years ago he had come visiting with his father. He remembered that Alhaji Biu had said something about purchasing the previous set of chairs from Paris. He wondered where these new sets of chairs originated.

A frown flickered across Jumai's face the moment she entered the living room. She had wanted to relax in the sitting room for a while but seeing Tanko in her house and on her couch, infuriated her.

She forced a smile. "Hello, Tanko."

Tanko was still thinking about the exotic chairs when he heard her surly voice. Somehow, it fueled his anger. "Hello? Just hello? Is that all you have to say to me?"

She shrugged and folded her arms. "I don't understand what you want me to tell you, Tanko. It's too early and if you don't mind, I have things I want to get back to accomplishing." She turned to leave. His very presence irritated her.

Tanko sprang to his feet. He angrily spoke in Hausa. "Are you okay? How dare you speak to me in such a manner?" He heaved a rapid sigh.

She hissed and ignored him. She replied in Hausa language, then spoke in fluent English language. "You asked for it. The last time I checked I am not yours or even married to you in real-time or in my dreams."

He sighed and rubbed his chin with a hand. "Is that the problem?"

Jumai wished she could slap his head. What exactly was wrong with the man standing before her? "What do you mean by that?"

"I mean the proposal." Well, my father is taking care of that." He assured her with a seductive smile. He stopped smiling when he scrutinized the tension on her face.

She sneered and shook her head in disbelief. "I'm sorry, Tanko. Is there any other thing your father will not be taking care of? Perhaps he'll also take care of the position you'll assume with your wife on your wedding night." Jumai's stinging remark made him grow pale with a perplexed look.

She noticed how irritated Tanko was and continued taunting him. "Perhaps, he'll help you take care of your manly duties with her as well." She feigned a shy smile.

Her words infuriated Tanko to the point he wished to slap her pretty little face. But she was a woman and most of all, the love of his life. He gritted his teeth. "I won't take that from you, Jumai. That's uncalled for."

She wanted to speak but clamped her lips tightly. She could see Tanko might not hesitate to raise his hand to her if she goaded him further. She flashed a meek smile and stared shyly at her feet.

When he saw that there was no retort from her, he

smiled, and his eyes turned soft. "Jumai, can't you see that I love you." His heartbeat at the thought of Jumai becoming a submissive partner. He wished that should be the case. Could she not see that he was madly in love with her? Or what guy in his right mind would leave work just to be with his wife-to-be.

She shook her head and spoke softly. "But I don't love you, Tanko. I expect you to accept this truth. It would be best for the both of us."

Jumai's rejection went straight to his heart and his being seemed to shatter into a million pieces. His eyes became moist. "Is that why you avoided me at the airport? I waited for you." He rubbed his hair in frustration. "Jumai, I never saw this coming. Do you hate me that much?"

"As you can see, I managed quite well. I don't need a footman. And I don't hate you. I can't simply be in a relationship with you." Her tone was firm, and she hoped Tanko would accept her stern decision.

He scratched his head and glanced briefly around the exotic living room. He noticed the phone in her hand. If he was not mistaken, she was holding the old iPhone, but he could always get her the latest iPhone brand. "But I don't want you to manage. My wife would never have to manage. May Allah forbid it. Give me the chance to prove myself to you. Let me make you the happiest woman in this country."

She wanted to slam it into his head that she was not a woman to be pleasured by an excessive display of affluence. "How do you intend to make me the happiest woman? Is it merely by your extravagant show of your father's wealth? Come on, Tanko, I was born in wealth, immense wealth. If you've been listening to me, you'll realize that I am looking for something deeper. Also, you're not even a man of your own."

His eyes turned red. "What do you mean by deeper? Are you saying I'm shallow?"

"I believe I've made myself clear on this issue; you can continue to assume whatever you may. Good day." She briskly turned to leave but Tanko held her by the arm. Jumai gasped in shock, she snatched her arm from his hold and cast a scornful glare at him.

She looked around the living room and became apprehensive when she noted nobody else was in sight. She blinked and tried to gather her composure. She blurted the first form of defense that came to mind. "You will commit *haram* in my own father's house? Are you insane?"

He gasped in shock and clasped his palms in apology. "I'm sorry, Jumai. I didn't mean to."

"Get out now before I call Yaro to throw you out." She

pointed at the door.

Tanko hissed in exasperation. He wished Jumai would grant him a comforting audience for him to prove his worth. He needed to be heard not pushed out like trash. He took a few steps towards her, but she stepped backward.

"Jumai, you just have to listen to me." His voice quivered. "Why are you being so cold towards me? I'm not a stranger. I'm not an ugly moron. Please, give me a chance to prove my love to you."

"Tanko, if you don't leave my presence this minute, I'll scream." She took some steps backward. "I swear to Allah, I'll scream."

His jaw dropped in disbelief. What did she mean by those words? Did she not know him and what he could do to her? He felt hurt and humiliated by Jumai's zero regards and trust for him. He slid his hands into his pockets and gritted his teeth. "I shall let this slide Jumai, but I want to warn you. If I find out there is more to these insults, I shall see to it, and then as Allah wills, I shall see to you." His eyes glinted dangerously, and the spark disappeared in a flash.

Jumai could recognize a serious threat when she saw or heard one, and she would be dammed if she took his threats lightly. She eyed him as he stepped out banging the front door. She slumped on the couch and tried to calm her racing heart but somehow, Tanko's stern threats kept finding a way to distort her thoughts. Aware that she was fidgety, she rushed out of the sitting room and mounted the stairs to her mother's bedroom.

Simbi was scrolling through her contact and was about to dial her friend's number when Jumai walked into her room as though she owned it. She studied her face briefly and knew that something must have suddenly gone wrong for her daughter to walk in with a disturbed countenance.

"Mom, I will not take this any longer. I really cannot stand it." She hated the way her voice quivered. It showed that she was still scared of Tanko's threats and she was not a weakling to chicken at mild threats.

Simbi dropped her phone on the magnificent bed. She sat up quickly in bed and patted a spot for Jumai to sit beside her. Jumai angrily folded her arms and remained standing.

"My dearest, what happened? I thought you went down to see your fiancé." Simbi watched as Jumai's face contorted into an irritated look.

"Tanko Taminu is not my fiancé and I'll appreciate it if you desist from calling him that. You are all making him more arrogant and it's irritating me like hell." She touched her head as if to ease the ache pounding within.

Simbi smiled. She recognized her resistance to Tanko's proposal. It was the same way she had felt when she was betrothed to Alhaji Biu. But now, she did not regret one bit of her union with her husband. She blushed knowingly. "I see. The lovers' quarrel has gotten the better of the two of you."

"Mom, that's far from it. It is not even close." Jumai scoffed. She stood and paced around the room. What was wrong with her mother? She was supposed to be on her side or try to calm her nerves.

Simbi chuckled impishly. "You're even more stubborn than I thought. Your father can't say that I didn't warn him. But Tanko is a very fine..."

"Mom." Jumai shook her head in disapproval. She was about to speak but a knock on the door interrupted her.

Fatima opened the door and peered into the room. She deeply inhaled the whiff of lavender mixed with a fruity smell in the room. She assumed that it must be from the scented candles Jumai had brought from abroad. "Mama Jumai."

Jumai sighed with relief upon hearing Fatima's voice. "Fatima, you're back." She was glad at Fatima's intrusion for it meant a pause to her mother's annoying responses.

"Yes. Why the long face? I saw your husband on my way out and…" Fatima paused when she saw Jumai's unsmiling face.

"What is wrong with everyone?" Jumai clenched her fists and stormed out of the room.

Fatima glanced at Simbi in confusion.

Simbi shrugged and broke into a wide smile. "They just had a lover's quarrel."

Fatima nodded shrewdly. She closed the door and went in search of her friend. She needed to hear about their lover's fight.

CHAPTER NINE

Yusuf's throat grew parched from thirst. He had been walking for a long time and he was far away from the village to knock on any hut and ask for water. Tiny beads of sweat formed around his furrowed brow. His face was stern, devoid of any emotions as to what was going through his mind. He stopped and tightened his hand on the bag when he saw a familiar truck driving towards him.

Yusuf's first intention had been to run away, but curiosity froze him on the spot. The truck stopped in front of him, and two hefty men alighted from the truck and gave Yusuf an aggressive look.

He clutched the bag to his hip and nodded at the men. Fate had led him here. If he had the guts to watch his daughter die, he could walk away and never look upon this path. He sighed at the drastic decision he was about to take for the sake of his sanity and family.

The men walked up to him and pulled out a black

coloured cloth. One of them blindfolded Yusuf with the cloth led him into the truck and jumped in after him. The truck began to move, and Yusuf felt his heart had stopped beating.

He was not sure of his next destination. The truck grounded to a halt and the men got him off the truck and guided him into a building. He made a fruitless effort to see the surrounding, but he gave up on the idea within some seconds.

He knew the feel of darkness when he was in one. The darkness was like the one at home, but the darkness in this strange place was deafening. Deep grunts alerted him to more company.

Yusuf could sense he was not the only stranger in the building. He could hear the heartbeat of other newcomers, and their silent question of what the future held for them. He sighed and listened to the dark for any further information he could decipher.

Yusuf heard unhurried footsteps come into the room. A strong fragrance wafted through the room and he denoted that whoever had stepped into the room had not been on the truck.

He was thirsty and hunger was digging a deep hole in his stomach. His knees buckled from weariness and he massaged his waist to suppress the sudden sharp pain he felt. He dared not speak because he could not tell if he would get water to quench his thirst or a dagger on his throat.

Danladi cleared his throat. "Blood for blood. Life for life. From here there is no return." Satisfied with the deafening silence, he strained his hoarse voice. "From here on, you join the brotherhood of men-In life and to the death." He noticed the uneasiness of the blindfolded men and gave a smug smile.

CHAPTER TEN

Zahra ignored the shrieking sound from the radio and focused on Jumai. She rubbed Jumai's back each time she had a jerking cough. She wrapped her arms around herself as a cold shiver ran down her spine. She wished there was something she could do to calm her fears. She could not bear to lose her grandchild. "I've not seen my son for many hours. Oh, Allah. Guide and always keep him safe. Save this widow from further tears."

The signal of the radio became clear, and the sonorous voice of a Hausa radio host filled the hut. The news of the Danladians going on a rampage across the city made Zahra's heart weak. She sighed and buried her head in her trembling palms. "Oh, Allah. Where is my son? Please, keep him safe and lead him home to me in one piece."

Heavy footsteps approached the hut and she looked up when she heard an unfamiliar voice. She flushed and raised her hands to the heavens in thanks. She quickly walked towards Yusuf but stopped when she saw the hefty man behind her son.

She appraised the man in a crisp black suit and her eyes

lingered on his well-trimmed hair. She glanced at Yusuf and silently asked for an explanation, but his blank expression left her with no clue. Zahra observed he was still wearing the same clothes and she became apprehensive. She wanted to ask him where he had been. but the man broke the silence.

"Madam I am Barrister Waheed Bello. Your son has been found worthy to work for our government." Waheed bowed.

Zahra gasped. Her son, who had been an unemployed graduate, was finally employed. She did a small dance of victory.

Yusuf forced a smile. His heart sank when he saw his mother's exciting dance. She felt proud not knowing her son had finally become a wretch.

"He will be working directly to execute government assignments in different states and countries. And as such, he may not return for the next 10 to 15 years."

Zahra became sad and slowly sank to the floor in tears.

Waheed opened his briefcase and took out a form. He squatted and presented the paper to Zahra. "Please, sign here."

She frowned and wiped her tears. "What sort of employment procedure is this? I'm not the applicant. Why give me a form to sign." She sniffed and her eyes widened. "Wait a minute, Sir. There is only one job that would need my signature." She gasped and hastily got to her feet. "I will not sign this paper." She beat her chest. "I may not have education, but I am not stupid." She wept bitterly. "You want me to use my hand and sign the death of my only son? Now take your useless self out of my house before I start biting you."

Yusuf rubbed his face with his palm. He had thought that his mother would not understand his kind of job, but it was evident that she knew the latest employment opportunities in the community. "Mama, you will have to sign it. Please, do it for the sake of my daughter." He joined his hands in a plea. "Mama, you need to make a choice. I tried all I could, but you can't have a son and a granddaughter in this lifetime. You must choose. And I've already chosen my daughter."

"I see you have gone mad. Where is your faith in Allah? Yusuf, I'm so disappointed. I never knew this day would come that I would have to remind you of your faith and trust in Allah. How can you just wake up one morning and decide to sell your soul to the devil?" She walked around Waheed, in bare feet, troubled and shaken. "We are hungry, yes. I need money, yes. But I will not sell my son to you

Danladians."

"Madam, let's quit the drama. Please, sign this document and put an end to your miserable existence."

She gave Waheed a malicious stare and turned to Yusuf and spoke calmly. "I know I was angry I had lost your father. I know I said a lot of things I did not mean. Yusuf, you must understand I said those things out of grieve and you should never have taken my words to heart." She made to hold his shoulder.

Yusuf moved backward and held up a hand. "Mama, just sign the papers and save Jumai for me. Please, I beg you in the name of Allah." He knelt and broke into heavy tears. "Please, Mama. If you truly feel my pain and love my daughter, then you have to do as I say."

Zahra glanced at her son and took the paper from Waheed. Her tears dropped on the paper as Waheed presented a box of ink for her to make a thumbprint.

CHAPTER ELEVEN

Yusuf and Waheed returned to the camp at night. A man ushered him into a dark room and switched on the light. The man clapped and left the room. Yusuf massaged his wrists and flexed his shoulder while surveying the room. The man returned with six other young men and asked all, including Yusuf to sit on the floor. A tall man walked into the room. His face was not as merciless as Inuwa's or the other men.

"Rise, brothers." Danladi's throaty voice resonated through the room.

Yusuf and the other men scrambled to their feet.

Danladi appraised each man and stopped to have an eye lock with Yusuf. He proudly spread his arms. "Welcome to the great fold of the Danladians."

Thereafter, Yusuf and the men were given their apartments in the camp. The camp was surrounded by great mountains. The houses were made of thatches and woods. One from a helicopter would never believe that those were houses. The leaves were so dry in the dry season which made it a good camouflage for them against security personnel hunting for them. Inuwa and Danladi had their rooms in the caves. Both held radios to their ears to be updated about the happenings in the world outside the cave.

Mosquitoes buzzed around Yusuf's ears and he cursed his fate for not being able to slap the blood-sucking creatures to death.

Suddenly, a soldier tied Yusuf's hands behind his back in order of deserving punishment. He let out his frustration with a deep groan. He had not had food and water for hours and the mosquitoes would not rest until they drained whatever was remaining of his blood.

Danladi touched his beard and chuckled. "You fought well today, Yusuf. I was really proud to call you my relative."

Yusuf gave a deep sigh. "I am not your relative."

Danladi smirked. "I'll pretend I never heard that." His eyes warmed over Yusuf's bare chest and arms. "I can understand your pain. Being tied up like a chicken set for the slaughter can be quite painful."

"Of course, you do." Yusuf gritted his teeth.

Danladi jammed his hands into his pockets and took a few steps closer to Yusuf. He stopped right in front of him.

"But you have to understand that there are rules guiding this place. There are strict rules which govern the things we do here. Without rules we are no different from the oppressive government we aim to replace. We cannot tolerate rebellion or disobedience."

Yusuf scoffed and thought this brotherhood was still like the oppressive government. It did not matter whichever way Danladi chose to look at it.

Danladi grinned evilly. "You need to understand that there is no communication with the outside world anymore. You are dead to your family and your family is dead to you."

Yusuf winced. He could not hide the fact that Danladi's words had pierced his heart. He wondered if he still had the heart to have joined the Danladians. He glanced sharply at him. "Was that not obvious in the memo?" He sneered and his smoke-dead teeth showed.

"I don't have to explain everything to you. There are things you must discover as a man. And there are challenges you need to accept as a man. This is your fate."

"Only Allah can decide a man's fate."

Danladi laughed with no trace of humour in his eyes or lips. "Oh, my dear nephew. Your razor tongue will never go blunt. But you're obviously a fool." He tugged at the ropes and freed Yusuf. "Be, good." He patted his cheek with aggression and walked away.

Yusuf rubbed his numbed wrists and shook his head. He looked around and stared at Danladi's retreating figure. He scoffed. "He calls me relative but did not have the common sense to bring me food or water." He hissed and lay on his back. "He is such a fool."

"I'll pretend I didn't hear that," Danladi called back before disappearing.

Yusuf grinned and closed his eyes in the hope a feast would be in front of him the moment he opened his eyes.

Early morning the next day, the ground was slippery from the rain. Yusuf and Garuba jogged through the forest with heavy boots that stalled them from slipping. It had become their routine ever since Yusuf joined the Danladians and Garuba was able to relive some good moments with his best friend.

Goosebumps gathered around Garuba's arms due to the cold. He rubbed his arms to simmer warmth into his body but stopped when he saw that Yusuf was far ahead. He raced while his teeth clattered from the cold. He glanced at his friend briefly and studied his dark features. Thin mouth, stoic face, and his stiff movements all communicated one thing to him, 'regret.'

The same regret he had felt when he first joined the Danladians. He understood his friend's countenance now but what he did not understand was why he had joined them. Yusuf suddenly lost momentum and slowdown in his pace. He stopped running and stood to catch his breath. He hid his face in his palms and sighed.

Garuba was able to meet up with Yusuf and stood to take a deep breath. He exhaled and took details of his dried singlet, unlike Yusuf's that plastered his body in sweat. He followed Yusuf's gaze and smiled upon the birds perching from tree to tree and understood Yusuf's reason for stopping. A wisp of freedom was the reason. They had forgotten what it meant to be truly free. They had been born free, but circumstances had put them in shackles for life.

"Why did you do this?" Garuba flexed his muscles and folded his arms. "I know you. I know you are a good man. I swear to Allah, Yusuf. I never thought you'd ever come here. I never wished you would. At least, unlike most of us, you are educated. You would've found a place in the city." He watched his friend wince from his last statement.

"It is easy to say, my friend." Yusuf turned away from Garuba and leaned into the baobab tree beside them. He had never found the right place in the city. Most of the job offers he got were not able to feed him a meal a day, still, he managed to do some jobs until he fell ill, and all his savings could not pay for a bed at the hospital. A gush of emotions rushed through him and his hands fell limply to his sides. The reality of being a Danladian weakened him. He suddenly wished that everything including his friend would fade into the background and everything would remain a thought that was unheard of.

Garuba cleared his throat. "You mustn't let these men perceive you as a bad investment. If you do not step up and carry out your mission with the utmost diligence, they will slaughter your family and everyone you hold dear to your heart.'

Yusuf heaved off the tree and squarely faced Garuba. "Nothing should happen to my precious Jumai and lovely mother. The only reason I'm here is for their well-being. I'll not have you talk ill of my family. If you ever do it again, I'll forget you are my best friend." His eyes turned red from un-shed tears. He wanted to say more but panic rang through his mind. His daughter was his life. He could not bear losing her to the dreaded sect.

"I'll not. I promise." Garuba said.

Yusuf turned around and jogged off. A dark sinister look enveloped his face. He was a Danladian now and there was no going back.

Danladi caught sight of the men going about their morning routine as they had been taught. A complacent smile played on his lips. Those men were a product of his belief and imagination of the right sources that would take up the reins of fighting for Allah.

He touched his beard absent-mindedly as a slightly distorted image of Yusuf briefly flashed through his mind. His smile extended into a dark grimace. He could recall the look he had seen on his face the last time they had talked. Yusuf had looked defeated and disappointed. He hoped Yusuf would not change his mind. He really hoped that would not be the glint of hope that had shone in Yusuf's eyes.

He chuckled and shook his head. "No, I don't think that would be the case. His new commitment would subdue him."

Inuwa eyed his superior and relaxed into the leather chair. He wondered what it was about Yusuf that made him special in the sight of Danladi. Surely, it could not be because of his strong body built or razor tongue. He just could not place it. And if there was anything he hated, it was having a competitor. He hated the guts of Yusuf. He sounded like an educated peacock; parading himself around the camp with that *haram* he calls an education.

Inuwa walked up to Danladi. "I don't feel right about Yusuf. He has the eyes of a traitor."

Danladi's gaze stayed on Yusuf. "Not at all. It's more like the eyes of a disappointed man. What you see is anguish, and anguish is good for the cause. He leaned into the chair. "He never expected to see me here."

Inuwa frowned and ransacked his mind on what Danladi meant by his last statement. He wondered if they had blood relations.

Danladi answered Garuba's silent question. "Yes, he is my nephew."

Inuwa's jaw dropped in surprise. "What? Are you a mind reader now?"

Danladi laughed at the funny look on Inuwa's face. "Close your mouth before you capture the whole flies in this area." Danladi laughed all the way through the darkroom to welcome recruits.

From that day, Danladi appointed Inuwa as Yusuf's instructor. Inuwa perceived it as an insult for Danladi to ask him to personally train his nephew. Was he trying to train his successor or what? He had loathed the idea, but he realized that the quickest way to get at Yusuf was to be closer to him. He engaged Yusuf in the art of throwing an opponent. In the wide arc, he put an arm in Yusuf's underarm and swiftly wrestled him to the ground.

"That's how to weaken your opponent or win a fight." Inuwa bellowed.

Yusuf groaned and slowly got off the ground.

"Did you see that?" Inuwa bellowed.

Yusuf nodded at Inuwa and focused on getting it right. He flexed his arm and keenly stared at Inuwa's bare torso.

Yusuf's training continued for weeks until he became an expert in defeating his opponent. Beneath the envy, Inuwa was proud that Yusuf learned fast under his tutelage. He became a minor instructor which was one of the highest and final stages to pass off as a Danladian.

Yusuf was taken aback when Inuwa handed him an assault rifle. He got used to training with a gun, but he never got to shooting from a distance to hit the targeted object. And so, he would line up behind Garuba and some others in a prone position with hands tightly gripping the assault rifle, and they would fire until their targeted objects became a successful hit.

Three months later, Danladi and Inuwa stood behind the men as they watched them run their tests by shooting from a range. Some of the men who failed their tests were taken back to the camp and whipped thoroughly for failing while the ones who passed were celebrated and approved for the next line of duty.

Yusuf stepped within range dressed in a black T-shirt, a checkered scarf tied around his neck, and pulled his assault rifle aiming at the object. He squinted an eye and placed his finger on the trigger. Determined that every action would take him forward at this point, he pulled the trigger, and the object came crashing down.

Some of the men around him chanted his name with pride. The cheers did not move Yusuf to bask in the glory of that great shot. He simply reloaded his weapon and attempted to take another shot.

Danladi's heart swelled with pride. It impressed him to know the training had made his nephew into a devoted Danladian. A proud smile played on his lips. He leaned towards Inuwa and whispered into his ear. "He is ready to take up any mission."

CHAPTER TWELVE

Alhaji Suleiman scrolled through some TV channels and flung the remote control on the couch. "Nothing interesting is showing. I hope lodging in this hotel is not a total waste. The subscription must be so cheap that no good channel is on the bouquet." He strolled over to his bed in his boxers with his protruding stomach peeking out of his white singlet. "I wonder what made me settle for such a useless hotel."

He lay on the bed, scrolled through his contact, and hissed upon the President's phone number. The event of the President's reelection bid flashed through his mind. He rolled on the bed and thought of ways to deal with the President for making that move.

He grinned sinisterly and closed his eyes. He opened his eyes and continued scrolling through the contacts until he got the name he searched for and dialed the number. He put the phone to his ear and waited for the receiver to take the call.

"Hello." A thick voice bellowed from the receiving end.

"Yes, the battle line has been drawn. I will use everything within my power to see him fail."

"Please, take it easy for the sake of our party."

He shook his head in dismissal of the call to caution. "I don't care anymore. If Mr. President wants war, I will give him a double dose of it. I will show him that he cannot bite the finger that fed him."

Alhaji Suleiman put his phone in his breast pocket. It had been a month since he and the President had had a face-off. He could hear Dimkpa, Alhaji Biu, and Alhaji Taminu's muffled discussions. He could note some comments on the next election. He heard them make references to his utterances at the last meeting and wondered if they would be loyal to the President in the tussle for the presidential ticket against him.

Alhaji Suleiman angrily stood and made his way out of the room.

"Alhaji Sule. Please, wait." Mairo ran after him. He stopped in front of a furious Alhaji Suleiman.

"How dare you, Mairo Zubairu?" Alhaji Suleiman wanted to remind him of his lowly background and how he had helped him join politics only to have ended up as a lap dog to the President. But he chose to hold his peace.

"Please. It's not what you think." Mairo's voice trembled.

"Then what is it? What is the true position? I am surprised you could bite the hands that fed you."

"I am loyal to you, Alhaji. And that's without a doubt. But all the party members at State and National level don't trust you." He watched as Alhaji's face contorted into hate.

Alhaji Biu and Alhaji Taminu exchanged glances and whispered amongst themselves.

Alhaji Suleiman nodded. He fisted his hands but could not afford to shut Mairo up with a punch. The media would only paint him as an unfit leader. He would have to let that comment slide for now. "So that is it."

"Yes. He is seen as Mr. Integrity. Only a monumental scandal on his part can alter the present situation. The action of the President towards you is raising lots of eyebrows." He dabbed his sweaty head and whispered. "There are lots of kin and kith behind him because they feel he's a man of integrity." He threw a glance at Alhaji Biu and back to Alhaji Suleiman.

"A man of integrity? Indeed, the world looks beautiful from afar. Now, I am painted red all of a sudden because I refused to compromise my status." Alhaji Suleiman looked crestfallen.

"Yes, a few of us are aware of that. But the President thinks otherwise."

The President's aide walked past them. He cast a curious stare at Mairo, and Alhaji Suleiman then briskly walked towards the car park.

Mario took his eyes off the aide and continued. "I am one of the few voices in your support but even that is inconsequential. Please, Alhaji, concede to the President's wish. We cannot afford to lose your verve and tact in the upcoming elections. We'd surely lose to Alhaji Barawu and the PPP. Please, I beg you."

Alhaji Suleiman hissed. "That would be over my dead body. And you can tell that to anyone who cares to listen." He shouted and bolted away.

Mairo's shoulder slumped in defeat. Alhaji Biu and the others walked past.

Alhaji Suleiman sighed with relief the moment his driver pulled out of the car park and into the road. His mind reeled with different thoughts. He had brief flashes of what had happened in the meeting. He sighed and relaxed fully into the seat.

He chuckled and spoke to no one in particular. "Can you imagine Mairo trying to sell me that cock and bull story? They think I don't know my party. I made the APP in this

Country."

He knew just what to do to all of them. He told the driver to turn off the music. He needed some quietness to re-strategize.

CHAPTER THIRTEEN

A car parked and Jumai quickly confirmed the driver's face and plate number matched the details on the Uber app. Jumai sighed with relief the moment she slid into the back seat of the cool Toyota Camry. It felt cool to be away from the scorching sun. It was on days like this she wished she drove in her car.

As soon as the Uber driver turned on the ignition, Jumai pulled out the chessboard she had bought from the mall. She studied the box, reading every label and inscription, and then she opened the box. She took the manual and opened it to the first page. She attentively flipped through more pages and smiled. If she must play chess, then she needed to know the chess' strategy.

The Uber driver tried to focus on the road, but he found himself glancing at Jumai through the rearview mirror. He frowned and concentrated on the road. His eyes gleamed and he stole glances at her again. His eyes took details of her pretty feature. He frowned again, took his eyes off the road briefly, and watched her pointed nose and full pink lips. It was not that they caught his attention in some sensual way. Her face told him another story, a story of familiarity.

He cleared his throat to put an end to his curiosity. "Excuse me, Madam. I guess you're Jumai." Bali Umar prayed his guess was right. He could not afford to irritate a random stranger with his question and open curiosity.

Jumai smiled warmly. "Yes, my name is Jumai. But anybody can bear that name."

Bali Umar blushed.

"I'm sorry, I do not…"

"I'm Bali Umar. I used to live next to you back in KD."

Jumai gasped. "*Wayo Allah*. Bali."

They exchanged pleasantries and discussed old times.

The taxi driver found a parking space and Jumai alighted from the car. She flung her head backward and laughed hysterically at what Bali Umar had said. After years apart, Bali Umar had still not changed his humorous style of diction and manner of approach.

***

Tanko and Simbi were in her living room chatting. Simbi was fair, slim, and had sexy cleavages. Tanko ignored the smell of Simbi's heavy cologne that made him dizzy and pleaded desperately. "I need you to help me convince her. I must marry Jumai. I will have it no other way."

He looked at the door in earnest and wondered where Jumai could be. He had thought he would meet her at home but was greeted with the news of her absence.

Simbi smiled and adjusted her gown. She understood young lovers. But she could not fathom why her daughter chose not to requite Tanko's love. "I shall talk to her. But most of you young men of today need to learn the art of wooing a woman. She says you're arrogant and bossy to her."

"I'm not, Mama. I'm only being a man she can be proud of. I want to be a man like my father, and her father. The kind of men you and my mother love and adore. I wish Jumai can see this and come to appreciate me the way I am."

Simbi nodded. "That is good. I see nothing wrong with that. You must be patient with her."

Tanko nodded. "I will."

Simbi felt an urge to encourage him. "As long as her father accepts you as his future son-in-law, there is no one else. Just you, Tanko Taminu." She smiled reassuringly.

Tanko swelled with pride and displayed an arrogant smile. He was about to stand when the newscaster's voice filled the living room with urgency.

'In the news...the Presidential aide was found dead, murdered in cold blood early today. Rumors are circulating the airwaves that his death may be politically influenced.'

Tanko punched his fist in anger while Simbi gasped in shock.

"When exactly would these meaningless killings end in the country? It is as if people no longer value the lives of other citizens." Tanko said.

They were still lost in the moment when they heard the main gates creak open. Tanko hurriedly got to his feet and spread out his arms to await Jumai's entrance into the house. Simbi smiled and went upstairs to her bedroom.

Tanko heard Jumai's laughter and let his arms down. It's been ages since he heard Jumai laugh. She had not laughed in his presence since her return. He grimaced. Who could be the source of her laughter? What exactly triggered her laughter?

He walked towards the window and saw her smiling with another man. He fisted his hands and angrily stared at the man. He was angry because Jumai had never granted him such deserving moments. What did that man have that he did not possess?

He had been craving such attention since the day she arrived in the country. Pain and anger flashed in his eyes and like a raging bull, he rushed out of the house towards Bali and lunged at him, punching his jaw.

The weight of the punch sent Bali crashing to the ground like heavy lumber. Bali writhed in pain and Tanko jumped on him to inflict more blows.

Jumai let out a piercing scream as she tried pushing Tanko off Bali. Tanko gathered Bali's front shirt in his hands and tightened his hold to choke him.

Simbi rushed towards them and yelled at Tanko. "Tanko, stop this madness at once."

Tanko hesitantly released his hold on Bali and rose to his feet. He turned to Jumai and glared at her. "You."

Jumai shuddered. She was certain that this was not the Tanko she used to know. This side of Tanko was scary. "Tanko, what in Allah's name is wrong with you?" She said in a faint voice.

His jaw tightened. "So, it has gotten to the extent of

messing around even in my presence."

"Messing around?" She scoffed.

Simbi helped Bali to stand on his feet. She lifted her head to mutter an apology to him when she froze in surprise. "Bali Umar?"

Bali gave a slight nod. His head pounded and his body ached.

"Tanko, he is an Uber driver and more importantly, an old family friend." Jumai sighed exasperatedly.

Simbi held Bali by the hand and nodded in agreement to Jumai's last statement. Another glance at Bali's swollen face made her heartache. "Jumai is right, Tanko. I know him. Please, spare him. I beg you. I know his family."

Tanko could feel perspiration in his underarms. The way he always felt whenever he did something stupid. Nonetheless, he cleared his throat. He would not give them a hint of how sorry he was. "Be careful, Jumai." His voice was stern. "I've got my body and soul on you." Tanko stormed off to his car and drove out of the compound hurriedly as though, he would be asked to apologize to the freaking Uber driver if he stayed a minute longer.

Jumai watched his car zoom off until she could no longer see his taillights. She stormed into the living room in fury and sat on the edge of the chair. She could not help thinking that Tanko had bitten more than he could chew.

Simbi apologized to Bali and went into the house. Bali took a long look at the house, got into his car, and drove out of the compound.

"This is the last straw. I won't take it anymore." Jumai paced around the living room.

"D'Allah, you have to calm down, Jumai."

Jumai turned around to face her mother. "Did you see what he did to Bali? Is that the sort of savage you and Baba want me to marry?"

Simbi shook her head and sat on the sofa. "Haba. He's not a savage. You have to understand the ways of men."

Anger clouded her eyes. "Don't even attempt to make excuses for him, mom. Tanko is the sort of fellow that will turn me into a punching bag when there is no one else to beat."

"Jumai, I admit he overreacted, but it's because he loves you. Not many men will enjoy seeing their wife laughing wantonly with other men."

Her face lit up with rage. "For the last time, I am not married to Tanko. And I'll never marry him." She hissed and stormed off to her bedroom. Everyone including her mother was pissing her off with the idea that she was already married to Tanko.

She flopped on the bed, wishing that the softness of the bed would drive drown her anger, but it still lingered. She rose to her feet, paced about, and sat on the edge of her bed. She knew of one person who could calm her. She picked up her phone and dialed Fatima's number.

Fatima had returned from running around her estate. Her innards burned despite entering her fully air-conditioned bedroom. She pulled off her shoes and got into the bathroom. Whilst bathing, she recalled the sexual rendezvous with her boyfriend from last night.

A small smile played on her lips. She placed her longhand on her chest and wriggled her buttocks wantonly. She softly scrubbed her body and rinsed it off. She came out of the bathroom with a towel around her body.

She was adjusting the towel on her upper body when her phone rang. She smiled on seeing Jumai's name displayed on her screen. She wondered what her friend wanted now.

"Jumai, how are you?"

"I'm fine. Can you imagine Tanko came to threaten me in my own father's house?"

She scoffed. "Threaten you? Why would your fiancé threaten?"

"Oh, don't even start with me." She yelled. "Don't ever call him my fiancé. I'll never marry that man."

Fatima giggled. Now she understood her friend's plight. "Relax, I'm only trying to get you to relax, you sound so stressed."

"Why shouldn't I be worried when everyone has married me off without my consent?"

She sighed. Her friend was right. "I understand that you're not yet in love with him, but you have to admit you've been a little rude to him of late."

"And that is because he's been hard at hearing me."

"Which also started lately? You were at least warm to him until you returned to the UK to complete your degree. I can still recall your rude response to him when he opted to drop you at the airport the previous year."

There was a brief pause on the phone. She rolled her eyes. "I'm no fool Jumai, I know you're not tripping for him anymore, but there are better ways. Tanko is not that bad. I mean we all grew up together." She tried to make her see reasons. At least if her little prep talk would cut off her pride then maybe everyone including Tanko would be happy again.

Jumai sighed. "Fatima, please just talk to Tanko. This dream he has will never come to pass." She said in Hausa.

She sensed her friend's frustration and smiled weakly. "I will talk to him."

"Thank you."

"Will you be at home tomorrow?" She caught sight of her underwear lying close to the door and smiled coyly at the memory of how it got there.

"Yes, I will. Come with Suya."

"Okay," Fatima looked up as soon as the door to the bedroom creaked open. "Bye." She added hurriedly and disconnected the call.

She shifted back her gaze to the man she had just shared a bed with. "You're back. I thought you had an important business to attend."

The man bowed and sauntered into the room. He looked up to find Fatima staring sexily at him. He gave a sly smile and walked up to her. He knew that his handsome body had a sexual effect on ladies, and she was not left out. "I thought of a more important business and came back."

Fatima tiptoed and excitedly kissed him on the lips. They fell on the bed and loved each other with feverish urgency.

CHAPTER FOURTEEN

The heavy structural presence of personnel of the Department of State Security, DSS, in Abuja guaranteed peace and security to all inhabitants, especially the elites. It was a quiet Monday except for cars moving in and out of the premises.

Ola sauntered into the premises and walked into the reception area where he paused to listen to what a cleric with a heavy turban wound around his head was saying on the television. A dark scowl etched on the cleric's face as he vehemently countered the state of insecurity from the interviewer.

"These pretenders are no servants of Allah and his prophet, peace unto him. They are the real infidels. Government should fish out these liars and murderous criminals. Every government agency should get on board no matter the cost." The cleric thundered.

Ola sighed deeply and walked out of the reception area. He could not hide his disgust at the recent happenings and the DSS' indifference to the fragility of the state in the hands of miscreants. The Danladians have proven to be a thorn in the city's roses.

He took the right turn and walked down the corridor that led to his office. He collided with someone and impulsively opened his arms to support the staggering figure when he caught a glimpse of her face.

"Aisha," he exclaimed. His eyes lazily roamed over her black t-shirt and black trousers and rested on her face cap. "You and your face cap. Can you ever leave it behind?" He chuckled and thought that Aisha Umaru would never cease to amaze him.

"*Oga Ola, báwo ni?*" Aisha grinned, flashing her perfect dentition.

Ola feigned being hurt. "Stick to your Hausa, your Yoruba sounds awful."

Aisha chuckled. "Alhaji is looking for you. He doesn't seem so happy."

"And does he think I'm happy? I'm fully aware of the implication of yesterday's disaster and I would have prevented it if I could." He stuck his hands in his pockets.

"I think he is looking for a scapegoat." She allowed her gaze to drift briefly to the brownish stain on the wall and then glanced back at him. "I guess Alhaji is looking for someone to transfer his aggression on."

Ola smiled weakly. "What about you?"

"Me? I had the common sense to stay out of the way. The way it is, we had better start detaining people fast, *wallahi*." Aisha placed her hands on her waist. She thought it was times like this she wished she were not a security operative but a simple woman with a regular job. But most times, she was proud of her career and glad to always be in active service.

Ola shook his head after evaluating her last statement. He cleared his throat and gave her a disapproving look. "We can't just detain people without evidence."

She shrugged. "Well, we need to act fast since unmasking the faces behind the Danladians proves to be an omen." She gave a satisfying smile. "Anyways, good luck arguing the constitution with Oga." She patted his shoulder as a way of solidarity to his future argument and walked away.

Ola sighed and rubbed his face with both hands. It was as if the whole weight of their conversation settled in his heart. He took another turn at the end of the corridor, which led him to his superior's office.

After a serious drill by his boss, Ola scurried to action with Aisha like hunters to arrest Suleiman as Biu instructed.

Ola smiled sardonically as soon as their vehicle pulled into the car park. He slowly got out of the car and pulled out his gun and other officers marched behind him, then spread out. Aisha pointed her gun at Alhaji Suleiman from afar.

Alhaji Suleiman became conscious of the intense eyes and weapon on him. He had considered his opponents would attempt to kill him, but he never imagined they could do it so soon and brazenly. He slightly turned around and noticed the supposed assassins were wearing the uniforms of some DSS.

Ola walked up to the puzzled Alhaji Suleiman. How he hated the sight of ruthless politicians. They were the root cause of terrorism and poverty in the country. "Zakari Dantata Suleiman. You are under arrest."

His heart stopped beating for a moment on the realization they were not here to kill him, but his mind began to race on the reason why they wanted to arrest him. "Arrest?" He shrugged nonchalantly despite his heart being in turmoil. "On what charge?"

"Terrorism. Now, you have the option of coming quietly or I shall have to apply reasonable force." Ola yelled. He loved scenes like this-Scenes where the powerful became powerless.

Alhaji Suleiman glanced at Aisha with many silent questions in his eyes. Her fierce face caused his lips to tremble. He sighed and raised his hands. There was no way he, Alhaji Suleiman would be publicly humiliated, and the perpetrators would get away with it. He consoled himself as Ola and Aisha closely escorted him to the patrol vehicle.

Alhaji Suleiman buried his face into his palms in the DSS' interrogation section. Madi walked into the room and glared at him. "Oga, sit well." He grabbed Alhaji Suleiman's shoulder and hoisted him to sit upright.

Alhaji Suleiman looked up. "Excuse me? What are you doing? Who recruited you as an officer? Is that the way to treat people and a dignitary at that?"

"*See, if I slap you, na for junction you go pick your teeth. Oga look me well o, I no like politicians.*" He yelled. "*If you try me, the wey I go use beat you, you go think say na motor jam you. Idiotic murderer.*"

The officer's outburst surprised Alhaji Suleiman. "Is this how you do your job? Calling an accused a murderer? Did I kill your mother or father? Did I kill you and it's your ghost standing in this room with me?"

Madi chuckled. "*Which job? Face front abeg, wicked politicians.*" He pointed at him. "*See, na every day I dey pray make God bring your type come here. I go beat you. I go wound you. I go...*" He raised his hand to hit Alhaji Suleiman, but the opening of the door stopped him.

Ola walked in. He glared at Madi and sat on the chair facing Alhaji Suleiman. "That's okay. You can leave now. Thank you."

Madi muttered inaudibly and walked out and shut the door behind him.

Ola grimaced. "I'm sorry about that." He sighed. "Your weapon was found at the scene of the crime."

Alhaji Suleiman lowered his head, and he studied his fingernail like they belonged to a stranger.

Ola cleared his throat. "The gunman you sent is now at large."

Alhaji Suleiman looked up and gave Ola a fierce look. "I sent no one. What on earth are you talking about? Your colleague was blabbering worse nonsense. This is some sort of joke. Officer, why am I here? You can't pin any crime on me. I'm a law-abiding citizen of this great country."

Ola jeered. "Really. And your gun?"

"My gun had been missing."

"Okay. Did you report that at any police station?"

"I never knew it was stolen."

Ola smirked again. "Typically, convenient."

Ola leaned forward that he was a few inches from Alhaji Suleiman's stoic face. "Listen to me and listen good Zakari Dantata Suleiman, this country has lost many people to the cruel shenanigans of men like you. Abuja has been looking for the faces behind the terror that this nation has witnessed in recent times. I am personally in search of such faces because I intend to deal cruelly with those faces. Now, if you don't want me to call in some of the boys, then I suggest you cooperate with me. Do you understand?" His uneven breath fanned Alhaji Suleiman's face.

Alhaji Suleiman relaxed his back on the chair and smiled weakly. "I want my lawyer."

Ola leaned back into his seat. He tilted his lip in a cunning smile. "Of course."

✳ ✳ ✳

"Hello." Alhaji Biu pressed the phone to his ear as he listened to the person on the other end. The car slowed to a stop and resumed with speed causing him to shift his weight properly on the seat. He continued nodding his head. "I see. That is good news. I'm on my way." He nodded. "This is really some good news."

He disconnected the call and turned to his friend who was engrossed in reading a newspaper.

"That scoundrel, Suleiman has been arrested on terrorism charges." He spread his arms and smiled. "Am I not impressive? The President had asked me to bring the sponsors to book and I have done it in less than three weeks he gave as an ultimatum." He patted his chest. "Wow, Alhaji Biu. Wow."

Alhaji Taminu shifted his gaze to his friend and chuckled. "My friend, how does that amount to your victory."

He shook his head and hissed. "Nonsense. Let's see our party deny me my right. Driver, turn the vehicle around. I need to see some people."

The driver nodded. "Yes, Alhaji."

CHAPTER FIFTEEN

The village was quiet with the birds busy building new nests. Dusk was fast approaching, and the girls deserted their routine of fetching water to witness the scene at the village centre.

The whole community seemed to have gathered around some Danladian soldiers. They unconsciously formed a circle around two youths who had received merciless beatings and were screaming in pain on the ground.

"*Wayo Allah*." Some people in the crowd exclaimed in Hausa as they watched the soldiers deal more blows all over the boys' bodies.

The boys bled so much they were near death. Inuwa stepped into the circle and raised a hand. The soldiers stopped beating the boys and retracted their steps. Inuwa appraised the boys' swollen faces and spat on them.

If there was anything Inuwa hated, it was a betrayal. And he made it known to the crowd. "These two have defied the sacred order of the brotherhood. After all, they had gained, they sought." He glared at them in utter disdain and turned to the people. "To abscond from their responsibilities, a crime that is punishable by death." He declared fiercely.

The crowd cheered in agreement while the youths trembled in fear.

Inuwa yelled and his eyes darkened with fury. "And death it is. Blood for blood. From here, there is no return."

The mob cheered loudly. A bearded man with a rifle made his way into the circle and there was perfect silence. His expressionless eyes made the crowd curious. He neither looked interested in defending the fate of the boys nor happy with their situation.

The boys buried their heads in the sand and wished the ground would split and engulf them. It was the best that could happen to them compared to dying at the hands of the bearded soulless man.

Yusuf ignored the attention he commanded when he walked into the circle and stroked his beard. Many people would not be able to guess the once innocent face of the man behind the rough beard. He pointed his gun towards the boys.

"Let this be a lesson to..." The bang of the gun dismissed the rest of Inuwa's words. He stared at the stilled bodies of the boys and smirked. The monster in Yusuf was finally out to terrorize their targets. He declared in his mind.

Inuwa watched Yusuf walk away to the admiration of the ecstatic mob who chanted in Hausa, "Brave soldier."

Garuba was quite shaken from what he had witnessed at the village centre. The dead boys flashed across his mind and the vivid state of what might become of him if he made a little mistake caused him to wear a forlorn look. He ignored one of the soldiers that waved at him. Yusuf's astute position of taking lives without blinking traumatized him.

He mocked as he briskly sauntered past the training ground. He wondered why the camp was unusually quiet. Garuba was still thinking about the expression on Yusuf's face when he stumbled on him.

Yusuf sat beneath a tree to clean his gun with a rag. A frown deepened across Garuba's face as he approached him. Yusuf deftly stroked his gun as if he was ready to kill at the moment. Garuba saw the bloodthirstiness in his friend's eyes. Where was his conscience? Did he suddenly lose it? "Yusuf, what was that?"

He stopped stroking the gun and laid it astride his thighs. "What?"

"How you murdered those boys like an unleashed beast.

That's what."

He chuckled softly and clamped his lips from barking out laughter. He shook his head and began to stroke the gun again. He looked pointedly at his friend. Was Garuba hallucinating? What were they if not beasts? "Are we not beasts? Blood for blood, an eye for an eye." He mocked. "Those are the words of beasts. That is what beasts are capable of doing."

Garuba shook his head. This was certainly not the Yusuf he used to know. "You never seemed like a man who would take another person's life."

He sneered, "That was when I still had a life." He kissed the gun and stared at it like a prized possession. "Now they have bought it, they control it. They own my life. Garuba, I sold my soul to the devil. I have proved my loyalty which was always in doubt even to you." He stood and stared point-blank at Garuba. "After all, we are all here to die."

Yusuf hissed and looked away from Garuba. He had to get away from this spot. His friend's presence was beginning to remind him of his old life. He shrugged, reminding himself of his new life; his current reality, and his expected future.

Ten minutes later, Garuba found him where he sat by the pavement along the dried river behind their camp.

He informed Yusuf that Danladi was searching for him. Yusuf wondered why he had sent for him. The last time he checked, he had not committed any crime. He rubbed his palms and cautioned himself to stop overthinking things. Danladi would have vital information, which was why he had called for him.

Different sizes of clothes clustered the room he shared with five men. He searched for his trouser amongst the pile of clothes on a chair. He grimaced, thinking how best to tell the men to grow up and not drag him into their mess. He was sure he had placed his trouser on his bag before going out for a run. He found the trouser and hissed. Yusuf buckled his trouser and wore his combat shoes. He looked around the room and went out.

Yusuf walked by some men and they stopped chattering. He ignored their inquisitive stares and whistled loudly. He got to the entrance of the darkroom and heaved a weary sigh. He never thought he would have to come to the room where recruits' fates were decided. The initiation room was a place he had hoped not to revisit. When the season of initiation was over, the darkroom served as the courtroom and Danladi's office. Yusuf stepped into the room and it took a while for his eyes to get accustomed to the dark.

Inuwa was standing by Danladi's chair. Yusuf stood in

front of them and braced his shoulder.

Yusuf nodded at Danladi. "You summoned me, Baba."

Danladi smiled. "Welcome, my son. Inuwa tells me you are far above your peers now. I am not surprised. I always knew you had the potential."

Yusuf's face remained stoic. "I am only glad to serve Allah."

Danladi played with the dagger on his desk. "Indeed. But tell me, Yusuf. Is that your true desire or is it because you feel you have no choice?"

Yusuf cleared his throat. "Our lives are now to further the cause."

Danladi exhaled. *Yusuf is a perfect soldier now.* He thought.

"Well said," Danladi beckoned to Yusuf to come closer. Yusuf nodded and moved close to Danladi's desk. "You have been chosen for a mission. It is a crucial one and a task that cannot be entrusted in the hands of mere soldiers. You are the most brilliant, efficient, and ruthless to carry out this mission. Are you ready?"

Yusuf raised an eyebrow. He wished his monstrous uncle could see the hatred hidden in his eyes. He gave a sly smile. "I have been ready from the minute you let your brother die of tuberculosis."

The words stung Danladi, but he quickly masked it with a blank face. He motioned for Yusuf to leave.

Yusuf sauntered out of the darkroom with a victorious expression on his face.

"Are you sure that boy is ready? He did not just exit a family meeting."

Danladi held a stiff hand. "Enough."

Inuwa clenched his teeth and fisted his hands so tight his veins popped up like thick ropes.

CHAPTER SIXTEEN

Tanko drove with a reckless spin of the wheel into Alhaji Biu's compound. He found a parking slot and slid out of the car. He looked a bit cool and collected in posture, but his eyes held this anger of breaking the Uber driver into tiny pieces.

He could not shake off the thoughts that Jumai and the driver might be having a romantic relationship. He was sure that if Jumai saw the driver as a neutral friend, the driver was having a more romantic idea of her.

He walked into the house and called out greetings, but no one answered. His eyes darted around the living room and across the dining area but there was no one in sight.

The thought of Jumai being alone with the Uber driver flashed through his mind. He conjured scenes of them romancing and he fisted his hands into tight balls. He glanced up the staircase and took the stairs two at a time. The only way to find out if Jumai was not with the Uber driver was to go up to her room.

Jumai had concluded her prayers but she was still on her mat. Tanko opened her bedroom door and strode in like a mad stray dog on the run. Jumai gasped and opened her eyes at the intrusive figure in her room. "Tanko, it is you. What is this?"

"You have not been picking my calls. Why?"

"Is that why you barged into my room like an untrained dog?"

Tanko fumed. "That does not answer my question."

Jumai rolled her prayer beads around her wrist and gently stood up to face him with an intensity that matched his rage. "I don't have to answer that. Leave my room, Tanko."

"Not until you tell me why you've been acting like a spoilt brat. Jumai, I demand an explanation and I'll not leave until I get my answers."

She glared at him and inhaled the sour smell about him. "You've been drinking." She derided. "So now, you're a shameless drunk. What a sorry excuse of a man you're. My parents should see you're not worth their daughter's hand."

Tanko could not bear being insulted and the disgusting way Jumai stared at him made him flinch with embarrassment. He slapped Jumai across the face. He staggered while Jumai fell on the bed and held her cheek in a daze.

He wriggled a shaky finger at her. "You've got to learn your place, Jumai. You must learn your place as my wife-to-be."

Jumai rubbed her burning cheek and stared at him with eyes filled with hate. "You slapped me."

"Why have you not been picking up my calls? Answer me." He yelled.

Jumai glared at him and defiantly tipped her chin.

"You treat me like trash. Do you know how many girls are dying to have me and yet I come to you and you treat me like trash? Why?"

Jumai shifted to the edge of the bed and pressed a hand on her bosom. She patted the space beside her and looked up at him. "Sit down, Tanko. Please, I'd like to explain some things to you." She batted her eyelashes.

Tanko's eyes were suspicious over Jumai.

Jumai sighed. "Okay, I admit I've been too hard on you. But I do all that in defense of your attitude. Tanko, your arrogance is overbearing. I wonder what I've done to you that you treat me like a piece of invaluable object."

"It's you. You keep on pushing me. Jumai, I love you. But you're making me crazy. You drive me crazy that sometimes I can't help myself. It's my love for you that makes me wild."

Jumai smiled and her voice softened. "Tanko, I do not despise you. I'm sorry for everything but you know us, women. We mustn't show our true emotions, or you'll take us for granted."

"I know, but…"

"Come, Tanko. Let's not argue anymore. Sit beside me."

Tanko smiled shyly. "I don't believe you." He eyed the bed and impulsively looked towards the window as though he was being watched. He glanced back at Jumai. "In bed? Are you sure?" He felt butterflies in his stomach. This opportunity was too golden for him to resist.

Jumai sighed impatiently. "Aren't you, my husband? Our parents deem it fit to betroth me to you so what can I do? I'm just a woman in a man's world." She clutched tight to the wedge shoe behind her.

Tanko's grin widened. His eyes flashed with a desire he had always had since he knew Jumai as an adult. He moved towards the bed and began to unbutton his shirt. Jumai beckoned on him to come closer. He smiled as he climbed over her, positioning himself so that he was a few inches away from her face. Her feminine cologne wafted through his nostrils. He inhaled deeply and groaned.

Tanko sniffed her neck to get more of her into his senses. "Allah. You're so beautiful." He shut his eyes and savoured the moment by biting his lip as his imaginations run wild with wants of seeing Jumai naked and plaint beneath his body.

"Kiss me. Kiss me." Jumai whispered as she allowed her breath to fan over his face. Her heart skipped fast in the realization of what she was about to do.

Tanko pouted his lips and came closer to Jumai.

Jumai gripped the shoe and hit Tanko on his head.

Tanko yelped and held his head. He removed his hand and gasped at the bloodstain. "Why did you hurt me?"

Jumai grabbed her phone and ran out of the bedroom. She hurried down the stairs in fright and frantically grabbed her car keys from the chair.

CHAPTER SEVENTEEN

Yusuf felt the car's tyres run on a smooth road and knew that they were miles from the village. He breathed a sigh of relief after a while and held tightly to his prayer beads. Yusuf caught sight of his reflection in the rearview mirror. He could not recognize the eyes that stared at him. He shook his head to ward off any streak of hallucination.

He stared at his long white *jalamia* and chuckled. He knew he looked ridiculous with the small white cap on his head.

Danladi's voice resonated to his hearing, *"what you are going to do requires planning and precision but insha Allah, I know you have the capability. You are the forefinger of the five and if you accomplish this task, we would have struck a blow that this government will find hard to recover. Are you with us to death?"*

He wished he had said no. But he would be a dead man if he had uttered such defiant word and his mother and daughter would be in grave danger. So, he said what he thought he should have said. *"To death."*

Yusuf did not realize they had reached their destination

until the gateman opened the heavy gates to an edifice of a hotel. Yusuf got down from the car and his eyes darted across the beautiful, mowed lawn. The attractive flowers around the fish-themed waterfall left him spellbound. He was glaring at the frangipani and coconut trees that stood in the compound when he saw a young man approach him. The other Danladians joined Yusuf.

"Welcome, Sir. I'm Maliki, at your service." Maliki bowed.

Yusuf and his colleagues nodded and allowed Maliki to lead them to the back of the magnificent white building.

Danladi's voice resonated in his mind again. *"You will undergo a process of purification at a chosen location. It is quiet there. You will cleanse yourselves there for ten days. Avoid communication with anybody. Focus on the task at hand. Allah is with you."*

✳ ✳ ✳

Jumai came out of the bathroom wrapped in the hotel's robe. She tied the towel around her hair and sat on the edge of the bed in deep thought. She hoped Tanko got medical help. The last thing she wanted was his blood on her hands. Instead of getting her way with her father, the police would be making their way to her. The vibration of her phone jostled her out of the unpleasant thoughts.

She picked up the phone and nervously stared at the caller's name. She sighed and answered the call. "Baba."

"My lovely daughter. Where are you?" Alhaji Biu said in a concerned tone.

"I am somewhere safe, Baba. I'll not come back home until you free me from Tanko Taminu." She sniffed.

Biu chuckled. "You have the temper of your father. Tell me my dearest. What happened?"

"It is better not said, Baba." She hiccupped.

"It must have been a big deal for you to break his head. And if you ask me, I'd say you went too far."

121

"What if he had killed me, Baba? He's lucky I could only break his head." She pouted.

He sighed. "I shall see you when I return from Abuja."

"I love you, Baba, but this is not up for discussion. I will not marry Tanko Taminu. And that is final."

Alhaji Biu chuckled. "When I return. Take care of yourself, my princess. I'm sure you will uphold your family's image in good light. Whatever you do out there, don't ruin our reputation. I'll not send a search party on your trail because you've been by yourself in the Western world, and you made us proud."

"Thank you, Baba. I'll be on my best behaviour."

"Great. Call me if you need more money."

"Okay, I'll, Baba. Bye." She sighed and ended the call.

Jumai changed into her nightclothes and got into bed. She took her phone and dialed Fatima's number. She smiled as Fatima received the call. "Hello, Fatima."

A few hours later, Fatima was in the hotel room with Jumai. Jumai threw her head back and her body shook in rhythm of her laughter. Fatima laughed as well, slapping her friend lightly on the shoulder. Jumai drew her shawl tightly around her slender frame. The security lights which lined the compound reflected on them and shone through the coconut trees that graced the compound.

Jumai stood with her back against the tree. "So, because you brought me dinner you won't let me rest."

Fatima giggled. "I didn't just bring you dinner. I kept you company in your prison. You're lucky you even have access to this place. I wonder why your father hasn't thought about looking for you here."

She shrugged. "I guess he's too preoccupied with his politicking to bother. At least he knows I'm safe."

"Your mom is worried. At least pick her calls." She sighed.

"And hear how it was my fault Tanko acted like a buffoon? No. I think I've had quite enough from Tanko's number one fan. Besides, she hardly picks calls too. I guess it's one of the traits I took from her." She had often told her mother to always be with her mobile phone and not toss it away like an insignificant thing in any part of the house.

Fatima chuckled. "My dear friend. You'll never cease to amaze me."

Jumai shifted her gaze towards the fence. She was about to look away when she caught sight of a person lurking at a corner of the compound in meditation. She wanted to get a glimpse of the person, but the purple hibiscus did well to shield the figure.

"Jumai."

Jumai broke out of her reverie and shifted her gaze back to her friend. "I'm sorry, what?"

"I said how long are you going to be here?"

She sighed. "As long as possible. Maybe until Baba returns and convinces me he has canceled the stupid engagement. But please Fatima, keep my whereabouts a secret. I don't need undue pressure from anybody."

She smiled. "I understand."

They talked for a while and laughed over some silly jokes.

Jumai placed a hand on Fatima's arm. "It's getting late. Fatima, in as much as I want you to stay with me like forever, I think you should get going. You can barely drive at night, remember."

Fatima nodded and hugged Jumai. "I'll miss you. Please, take care of yourself."

Jumai saw Fatima off to her car. She waited until the car was out of the gates before turning around to head to her room. She stopped and walked back to the area of the purple hibiscus.

She frowned. "This is strange. I could swear I had seen a man bent over here in meditation." Jumai shrugged and briskly leaped into the building with the thought of the meditating stranger on her mind.

Jumai put the empty food packs and bottles in a plastic bag. She scampered towards the trash can which was just beside the window and dumped the plastic bag in it. She moved to adjust the blinds when she caught sight of a mat tucked safely beside the flowers. She craned her neck to get a better view. She frowned and rushed out of the room.

CHAPTER EIGHTEEN

Yusuf returned to the flower area, took his mat, and spread it on the ground. He knelt and began to pray with his beads. He shut his eyes in deep meditation and clamped his lips. A gentle breeze ruffled the flowers, and he inhaled the fragrance. He loved the ambiance of this place. The peace and quietness calmed his soul.

"Hello," Jumai said with a radiant smile.

Yusuf opened his eyes and glared at a reflection of a goddess. He held his breath and wondered if Allah had sent his reward even before he executed the mission. Her beauty awed him, but he thought he had to earn this honour. He shook his head and willed her to disappear and reappear at the opportune time.

"I'm sorry for disturbing you. I saw you when I escorted my friend to her car. You went away before I had an encounter with you. Now you're back. You're meditating."

Yusuf gawked at Jumai and shook his head to clear out the reverie. He had not seen an Angel, after all. It was flesh and blood in front of him.

She folded her arms and eyed his prayer bead as though wishing that she was in the same position as the bead. "Are you a holy man?"

Yusuf nodded. Her beauty made him speechless.

She clasped her hands with a mischievous grin on her lips. "Are you dumb?"

He scoffed. "What sort of question is that?"

"Aha. So, he talks." She rolled her eyes at him.

"Of course, I talk. Whatever gave you the impression I don't?" He found it embarrassing to be called dumb.

She threw him a wry look.

Yusuf looked at his wristwatch and stood up. He did not want to have any involvement with the strange lady.

Jumai chuckled. "You really should talk more."

"Maybe I've learned that talking never helped much."

"Perhaps. But we've never met before and one might consider your silence as rude." She was not sure of what clouded his eyes. She had her guess between arrogance and prejudice.

"You really shouldn't be talking to strangers, young lady."

"Jumai."

Yusuf's heart skipped. "What?"

"Jumai. My name is Jumai." She smiled.

Yusuf took a step forward. He recalled some moments with his daughter and held back a cry. He stepped back and nodded. "That's a nice name. Do have a splendid day." He made to walk away.

Jumai spread her arms. "Are you going to walk off like that? Common custom requires you to tell me your name."

Yusuf turned around with a dark scowl on his face. "I won't tell you my name." He yelled.

Jumai gasped and moved backward. "Is anything the matter?"

He shook his head and looked up at her. "You shouldn't be talking to strangers, Jumai." His voice softened as images of his daughter flashed across his mind.

"Really?" She fought back a smile.

"Yes. It's. It's what I'd tell my sister." He stammered.

"Well, I'm not your sister and you aren't a stranger. You're a holy man. And you don't look like one that could hurt a fly." Her eyes lazily roamed over his white garb.

Yusuf quirked an eyebrow. "Oh."

Jumai smiled. "I know because I'm a good judge of character." She folded her arms and shifted her weight to one leg. She did not want this moment to end. She had not had a lively conversation for a while now.

"I see. So, you don't think I'm a blood thirsty terrorist?"

He could hear his heartbeat softly.

Jumai giggled. "You're funny. I guess next, you'll tell me you're a Danladian?"

Jumai's utterance took him by surprise. He looked uneasy and wiped off the sweat gathering on his forehead. "I, I'm not…" He stuttered and clamped his mouth shut. He heard a loud whistle and turned in the direction of the sound and saw Kawu beckon at him to come over.

Yusuf shrugged. "Well, it is nice meeting you. Excuse me. I need to pray now."

Jumai smiled. "Of course. Maybe we'll chat later." She said with a tinge of disappointment.

"I doubt your husband would like that." He gave a slight nod. He was eager to leave. He did not want her in trouble, at least not after hearing her name.

She gave him a stern look. "I'm not married and please don't ask me what a single Muslim girl is doing alone at a Guest House, thank you."

He sighed and rose to his feet. "I won't. On a serious note, you really shouldn't be talking to strangers. Goodnight, Jumai." He picked up his mat and walked away.

Jumai played with her scarf as he walked away without looking back at her. She sighed and headed to her room. She scanned the corridor before closing the door and sat on the edge of the bed. She crossed her legs and stared at nothing in particular.

Brief flashes of her conversation with the holy man ran across her mind. She recalled that he had skin as brown as the favourite chocolate she always bought at the mall and eyes as dark as charcoal. She also recalled how sensual his lips were and she could not help but notice his huge muscular frame underneath the flowing garb. She lay on the bed and dreamily stared at the ceiling.

CHAPTER NINETEEN

The road was observing its everyday routine of impatient motorists and passersby hurrying to their various destinations. Ola eyed the bushy path he had parked his vehicle and smiled. It was the perfect spot for what he had in mind.

The busyness of the road would not make random people pay heed to his business of the day. Aisha had warned him that this exercise should be worth the time and he would make sure to blow her mind with his tactics. When he saw her glance at her wristwatch for the umpteenth time, he knew he had to calm her nerves.

"You have to stop doing that. We're on a job." He smiled.

"But you haven't told me why we're here. We've been waiting here for the past two hours. Arsenal is playing." She hated spending long hours on the road with Ola only to return to base with no clue.

Ola grinned. "You should be glad you're not viewing the match. Arsenal always disappoints."

"It's not your disappointment." She retorted.

He chuckled. "Be patient." He stared at his watch. "I'm waiting for one of my eyes."

Aisha raised an eyebrow. "Your informant?"

Ola nodded.

Aisha nodded and gave him an impressive smile. "Something's about to go down?" She fiddled with her phone.

He whispered. "That's why we need to be patient. You can go on the internet to check the scores of the match. I don't want to turn on the radio to avoid distractions." He glanced at the side view mirror and saw a blind man with a young guide holding his arm. He turned to Aisha. "Don't say a word."

The blind man stopped by the window, tapped on it, and begged for alms. The young guide placed a hand on the window.

Aisha stared at the young guide before shifting her gaze on the blind beggar.

Ola took some naira notes from his pocket and put them in the beggar's hand. The beggar and his guide thanked him in Hausa language and walked on to the next vehicle.

Aisha held his arm. "Hey. What just happened?"

"I got the info I needed. The Danladians are planning a strike in a few days." He nodded as Aisha's eyes widened.

She shook her head. "And how did you know that? The blind man never said or gave you anything."

Ola chuckled and winked at Aisha. "Whoever said the blind man was my informant?"

She frowned and her eyes widened as the impact of his words hit her. "Oh, no. You did not…"

"I say a Big Yes to whatever that's running through your mind." Ola chuckled and started the car.

CHAPTER TWENTY

It was a quiet night. The stars' huge display brightened up the whole arena. Jumai allowed the cool breeze to caress her face as she wrapped her arms around her midsection. Her woolen shirt thinly protected her from the cool breeze that swept the vicinity. Her gaze shifted towards the corner of the house and her eyes caught a familiar view. She strolled towards the corner and found the holy man she had seen the other day.

Jumai muffled a laugh as an idea crept into her head. She noiselessly tiptoed towards him. "You never told me your name."

Yusuf frowned. "You shouldn't do that, young Jumai. Your fragrance gave you away. At first, I had thought the footsteps were that of an enemy. My dagger was ready for battle. Please, it's dangerous to creep up on anyone like that. Don't ever do that again."

"No, it's just Jumai. Not young Jumai." She smiled wryly.

Yusuf sighed. "It looks like you have a lot of free time

on your hands."

She shrugged. "Maybe. I'm on some sort of vacation."

He grinned. "A sort of vacation?"

She folded her arms in a defensive posture. "Yes. Is there a problem with that?"

He quickly clasped his hands. "Jumai, have you ever considered leaving the life of sin over living a holy life?"

She stared at him. Her smile faded to a petulant pout. "Are you insinuating I'm a… What do they call these girls again? Ah, yes. A slay queen or runs girl?"

He frowned. "I didn't say that."

"Then what do you mean by that offensive statement? So, I'm a sinner because I'm at a Guest House alone? What if it belongs to my father? Perhaps, you think I'm too poor to pay for a room without the aid of some Alhaji. Maybe you are one of those chauvinists that believe we women should be locked up in the room." She was too angry to notice Yusuf's wry expression.

He cried out exasperatedly. "Allah. You talk too much."

She assumed a defiant stance. "Oh, now I'm talkative."

Yusuf shook his head and yawned.

"Well?"

"Well, what?" He asked softly.

"Are you not going to say something?"

He shook his head. "I'm almost afraid to say anything now."

She sighed. "Good. A wise man knows when to apply silence. I'm going to bed."

"Okay. Goodnight."

She glared at him. Was that all he had to say?

Yusuf frowned in confusion. Had he said something wrong again? "What? Is goodnight the wrong thing to say too? What do you want me to say to you?"

"Your name."

He sighed. "Yusuf. My name is Yusuf Ibrahim."

She nodded. "Goodnight, Yusuf Ibrahim."

Yusuf heard her giggle and said his name like three times before she went out of sight.

❈ ❈ ❈

Tanko could not tell if the chairs in the living room were the same colour as it was. He would have been able to recollect every detail if only his head did not ache as much as it did now. Jumai's shoe had put him in a lot of pain. It was his love that had made Jumai a living soul. If it had been any other person that assaulted him, the person would be minced meat by now.

Simbi felt sorry for the young man. He looked miserable from the wound on his head and Jumai's disappearance. She never knew the extent of the damage her daughter had caused until now. "I'm sorry, Tanko. I've tried several times but she's not picking up my calls. I've called Alhaji and he told me to be patient until he comes back from Abuja."

Tanko sighed. "I'm in pains, Alhaja." He touched his head and winced in pain. "I know I've offended her. I'll do anything to seek her forgiveness. Anything."

"I know."

"But I don't think she'll ever forgive me."

She sighed. "Let's not lose faith, Tanko. I know my daughter. She is spirited but she has a good heart. Look, why don't you discuss with your father to speed up the marital rights? I think when she formally becomes yours, she will come to love and respect you. Right now, she might be feeling out of place in all these relations. It could be overwhelming for her."

"I've discussed the marriage preparation with my father, but you know they're pre-occupied with the upcoming primaries. It means a lot to both Alhaji and my father." He said helplessly.

"That's true, my dear." She nodded thoughtfully.

A few moments later, Simbi walked him off the house, and he got into his car. She bade him farewell and returned to the house.

Tanko honked the horn and pulled out of the compound. He saw Fatima in a cab and stopped outside the gates.

Fatima paid the cab fare and took a bag from the back seat. He glanced at the overnight bag in her hand. "Hey, Fatima." He hollered and winced at the pain that shot up in his head.

Fatima smiled and clutched her handbag to her side. "Tanko. Hi."

"It's been a while, what's up?"

She gestured towards the house, "Nothing much. I've just been busy. I came to see Alhaja."

He looked at the handbag again and nodded. "I see. Well, I've been meaning to tell you something. I have a friend that gifted me the latest iPhone. I have no use for it. Do you want it?"

She jumped in excitement and closed her hands over her mouth. *Wow. I would do the possible to have the phone. This is a dream turning into reality.* She ignored the other thought about doing anything that would jeopardize her friendship with Jumai. She shrugged and pushed the thought aside. Tanko loved Jumai very much and would not want to do anything that would hurt or disrespect her.

Tanko grinned. "I'll let you have it the moment you grant a little wish of mine."

Fatima smiled knowingly and came closer to the passenger's seat of his car.

CHAPTER TWENTY-ONE

Yusuf headed to the courtyard and called out greetings to the soldiers he passed by. A soldier offered him coffee from his cup and Yusuf declined with a smile. He needed a breath of fresh air and since he could not embark on his long morning run, a nice morning walk would suffice.

He was barely out of the building when he sensed some footsteps behind him. His hand moved to the dagger in his pocket and clutched it.

"Good morning, holy man Yusuf Ibrahim," Jumai said excitedly.

Yusuf released his hold on the dagger and sighed. He turned around and beheld the lovely figure accentuated by the trouser and chiffon blouse. He wanted to shove her inside or use his garb to cover her obvious features. He sighed again and focused on her radiant face. "Good morning, Miss Jumai."

"Jumai. Just Jumai." Jumai blushed and played with the hem of her top.

He nodded. "Good morning, Jumai."

"It looks like you're not happy to see me this morning."

"I never said that."

Her face lit up with a smile. "Good. Are you hungry? Have you had anything to eat?"

"I'm fasting."

"Oh. I'm sorry I asked. I had no idea. I beg your pardon, holy man."

Yusuf raised an eyebrow.

"I guess fasting, and the holy man should be one in spirit. I wish you well." Jumai dusted off a speck of dust off her wrist and stared at Yusuf from beneath her eyelashes. "I think you don't like being around the opposite sex."

He frowned. "Why would you say that?"

"Well, for one, you can barely look me in the face. Then you tend to stutter whenever I'm in your presence. There is this look you want me gone even before I come close. You're not behaving like a man my Fatima would call a 'sharp guy." She scrutinized his face, but he would not give away any emotion.

He shook his head and stared at his feet. "Maybe I'm not used to beautiful ladies walking up to me."

Jumai grinned and stared at his lips. She wished he could repeat those words. He looked up and saw the glow on Jumai's face. He felt satisfied that he had made her smile. Jumai cleared her throat several times.

"Do you want to say something?"

"You called me a beautiful lady. So, you do have a liking for me." She rolled her eyes at him.

"What?" Yusuf looked around him and chuckled. "I guess there is no winning with you. So, I wouldn't start." A voice played in his head to tread carefully and have his emotions intact.

Jumai giggled. "Wait a moment, I'll be back." She ran off

Kawu walked towards Yusuf. "She's a very beautiful lady."

"What?" Yusuf looked around. "Who are you talking about?"

Kawu held Yusuf's shoulder. "Brother, it's too late to act smart. I watched you with the lady."

"Oh, Jumai." Yusuf shrugged. "Yes, she is beautiful. She would have made a very good companion. But Allah has decided otherwise it seems."

"I'm glad you are aware of that. Be careful, brother. The others were worried you had lost focus. Remember the instructions. Remember what is at stake if you lose your sights on this mission."

He smiled. "She's nothing, just a silly little girl. We are also advised in our training to blend in to avoid suspicion,

Kawu. That's what I'm doing. You can tell the others they should save their worries for their waiting virgins." He chuckled.

Kawu chuckled. "Bastard. Very well, brother. Be careful." He playfully hit Yusuf on the back and walked away.

Jumai returned with a chessboard. She smiled and held out the game to Yusuf. "So, do you know how to play this game?"

The sight of the chessboard jolted Yusuf to his past. Blurry images of him playing chess with his daughter and Garuba flashed through his mind. His past was a powerful shadow; it would follow him anywhere, at night and by day. He reached out to take the chessboard, but his fingers grew numb. He sighed and turned to leave.

Jumai frowned. "Hey, don't walk away like that. I could teach you." Jumai watched him walk away with a stiff gait. She scoffed, "what a sore loser. He gave up even before the game began."

Yusuf grinned at her statement. As he took slow steps towards the courtyard, he strained his ears to catch more of Jumai's whining.

Jumai shrugged. "I just wanted to play a harmless game with him. He walked away as if it would ruin him fast.

What a weird guy." She grunted and went back into the building.

Yusuf could not stop grinning as he ran around the courtyard.

✳ ✳ ✳

Cool breeze whizzed by as Yusuf knelt on the mat to offer prayers. He looked to the sky and made some chants. He concluded his prayer and took a deep breath.

"Did I offend you in any way?" Jumai said in Hausa and crouched beside him on the mat.

Yusuf sighed and held tight to his prayer bead. "No. Well, the chessboard reminded me of something I want to forget." He smiled.

"Do you play then?" She sat on the mat and stretched her legs.

He nodded.

"Tell me about yourself."

"What is there to tell? I am sold out to a new cause. I have chosen for life and in that there is no return." He said absentmindedly.

Jumai's eyes were dreamy. "Have you ever wondered why I pester you?"

"Because you are a pest? Well, I'm beginning to get comfortable with your presence." He chuckled.

She grinned. "I perceive you are a man of deep principles and have a lot of respect for women. I admire that in a man. You're the sort of man I haven't come across in a very long while. Trust me; the Western world has a lot of shallow people."

"You honour me, Jumai, but you mustn't. I am just an inconsequential holy man on a path to purity." He smiled shyly.

"I understand, but even holy men are not impervious to affections of those who truly admire their altruism."

He sighed. "I have a feeling you'll be the death of me."

Jumai threw her head backward and laughed out loud.

Yusuf wished to place his lips on her throat and suck on it. He quickly recoiled from watching her laugh and cleared his throat. "I graduated from school and couldn't get employment. I did several odd jobs before I had to return to take care of my ailing father. He died." He lowered his gaze to his prayer beads.

She gasped. "Oh, Allah."

"We give Allah all the praise."

"I'm sorry about your loss. It seems you've been through a lot more than your eyes and words give away."

"I have, but Allah sustains me. He's made a way for me eventually."

Jumai stared at Yusuf in open admiration. How could he have gone through a lot and yet remained unshaken? She felt shy all of a sudden. She was getting to like him and his simple yet, principled ways. "Do you have a phone that I can reach you on?"

He shook his head. He should stop himself from speaking but with Jumai, he seemed not to think before speaking. "I am not allowed to own a phone, to avoid distractions."

She nodded. She needed to be in her room, far from his magnetic allure. "I have to go now, Yusuf. I shall see you later."

He wanted her to stay so that he could get lost in her beautiful smiles, laughter, and carefree dispositions. "Okay. See you some other time. I would love to see you again." He said the words aloud thinking they were rumbling somewhere in his thought.

Jumai gave him a radiant smile.

"Come by my room tonight. I want to show you something." He added.

She wondered what he wanted to show her. But whatever it was, she already liked the sound of it. "See you, then. Bye." She got up and took her leave.

Yusuf could not take his eyes off her. If hearts could be told who to develop feelings for, he would have told his heart not to fall for Jumai. She could be the death of him. He folded his mat and went back to his room.

✱ ✱ ✱

Jumai knocked on Yusuf's door. It seemed he had been waiting on her because he opened the door before the knock's echo receded. He held her hand and took her to the balcony. He wished he could wound his arms around her and stare into those beautiful eyes and tell her how much his heart pined for her. Her beauty mesmerized him each passing day.

"This is so beautiful." She gazed longingly at the stars. She wished she could get lost in them with Yusuf.

He stared at her with longing. "Yes. I wanted you to see it. I had a feeling you hardly take out the time to admire this beauty."

She met his gaze and blushed. "You are full of surprises." She sighed. "I don't even know what to say or how to tell you this, Yusuf." Her heart skipped. "But I don't care." She fondled the scarf around her shoulder.

"What's the matter? Is something wrong?"

"Yes. Everything is wrong. When roses suddenly turn blue, then everything is wrong. When the sun hides behind the clouds permanently, then everything is wrong."

He frowned. "I wish I understood your words. I'm lost in their depth. What are you trying to say?"

148

She bit her lip. "My father betrothed me to a man."

Yusuf clenched his fists. He nodded. "Yes, go on."

"But I simply have no iota of affection for him." Her hands trembled. "The pressure is killing me and I have fought it off for so long. I simply can't see a future with him. He's so shallow, so full of himself. But he is the son of my father's best friend and I have a duty to the family. That's why I'm here. I practically ran here when he became unbearable."

Yusuf frowned. "What do you want to do then?" He clenched his teeth in anger. Men like Jumai's betrothed deserved death and nothing more.

"I do not know, Yusuf. I am tired. My will is breaking. I don't have a say. I'm expected to fulfill my parents' wish. Nobody cares about what I want."

He sighed. "Your will is yours, and it's within your right to do whatever pleases you. You have that much privilege."

"But I'm alone in this."

"You are enough. I see strength in your eyes, Jumai. In your beautiful eyes, I see the strength of a lioness who commands the will of those around her. Such a will cannot be weakened or subdued, it can only grow stronger. You will prevail only if you let the world see that you shall not be anybody's pawn." He was tempted to applaud his speech. Where was this speech when he needed it?

"Do you believe so?"

"Yes, I know so. It's in you."

Yusuf felt a cold touch on his arm. Fear gripped him but he relaxed when more fingers began to caress him. His heartbeat continued widely and his head ached a bit. "Relax; I just want to feel you," Jumai whispered.

The way Jumai paid attention to the stars mesmerized him. He looked away from her and luxuriated in the act of trying to count the stars.

CHAPTER TWENTY-TWO

Tanko did not pay attention to the passenger seated next to him. His friend could yank off the compartment lid he held onto for all he cared. He drove beyond road safety's speed limit and grinned roughly. All that mattered to him was getting to the guesthouse in time to see his heartbeat.

He could not stand another day without seeing or hearing from her. His hands clung tight to the steering wheel as he took a sharp turn that led to his destination. He honked the car's horn repeatedly until the gateman opened the gates. He drove in and got out of the vehicle before his friend could catch his breath.

Tanko bounded up the stairs and thought why Jumai was lodging in a hotel unaccompanied by a female friend or family member. *How could she stay in a place with less security?* Did she not know the daughter of whom she was? As soon as he ascended the last stairs, Tanko saw Jumai at the landing. His eyes roamed over her and settled on her modest gown. He sighed in relief on seeing she was decently clad. He wanted to tell her that she looked beautiful, even prettier than the last time he had seen her but the hurt in his heart restrained him.

"I do not understand why you defy me at every turn. It is becoming irritating, Jumai. You hit me and left me. And then you ran off without telling anybody where you were. What if I had died?"

"I'm sorry for the injury, Tanko. You left me with no choice. I have told my father to cancel the engagement and I'm sure he'll do that on his return from Abuja."

Jumai's words took him by surprise. He had thought that hitting him would make her feel remorse on seeing his hurt countenance. He had dreamed that they would kiss and make up. "But your life is to live for mine. You are my betrothed, Jumai."

She shook her head and raised her hands. "But I am not your slave. I will not become just a trophy to hoist before your family and friends. I am sorry, Tanko. I will not marry you at any cost."

He took two menacing steps towards her and wagged his finger to her face. "How dare you?"

Yusuf was heading up to his room when he saw Jumai and Tanko at each other's throats. He frowned on seeing the lanky man speak threateningly at her. In a few long strides, he strolled over. "Hey."

Tanko and Jumai turned to look in Yusuf's direction.

Jumai sighed with relief on seeing him. Somehow, she knew that his presence brought some kind of peace around her.

Tanko had a denigrating expression on his face. "And who is this donkey?"

"Tanko," Jumai said in a warning tone. If she knew anything about body language, it was that Yusuf's calmness should not be mistaken for weakness.

Yusuf clutched his prayer beads in his palm. "I am not a donkey and I warn you to be careful about your choice of words before a holy man. You are disturbing the peace of this place and you are troubling the lady." He spoke stiffly. But his unctuous voice seemed not to have any effect on Tanko.

"And since when do holy men interfere in the affairs of married couples?"

Yusuf jeered and bit his lip in a taunting smile. "You are not married to her and even if you were, I must insist that you are not a man worthy of the love of such a woman."

Jumai gasped.

Tanko's eyes widened, and his nose flared in anger. He balled his hands. "Why, you fool."

Tanko made to strike, but Yusuf deftly stepped aside, his foot locked Tanko's at the ankle and swept him off his feet so that, Tanko flipped in an arc, and falls face flat to the floor.

Jumai beamed. Her eyes widened and her heart continued to beat more in admiration for Yusuf who was still standing and not panting or breaking into a sweat like the sore loser, Tanko.

Kawu and another warrior watched the action. The warrior rose to help Yusuf but Kawu halted his actions.

Tanko's fall was a huge embarrassment to his personality. He felt empty after Yusuf defeated him in Jumai's presence. "You did this to me."

"If I were you, I'd pretend this never happened. It isn't wise to let people know the mighty arrogant boy was defeated by one humble holy man. Now leave." Yusuf said sternly.

Tanko scrambled to his feet and gasped in anger.

Jumai feared that Yusuf would beat Tanko beyond recognition if she did not do something. She stepped in between them. "Tanko, I think you should leave. Please, I beg you in the name of Allah."

Tanko glared at Yusuf. "I will remember this insult. I swear to Allah."

Yusuf smiled while Tanko stormed out of the building, got into his car, and furiously drove out of the compound that the gateman jumped aside to save his legs.

Jumai gave a slight nod to Yusuf in gratitude. He nodded and hobbled away.

CHAPTER TWENTY-THREE

Jumai tossed and turned in bed. She grabbed a pillow and dreamily cuddled it to her bosom. She would not stop thinking about Yusuf and his raw courage to take on anything or anybody.

She stared at the ceiling and blushed. "I think I've fallen in love. The thought of him keeps me awake. And whenever he happens upon my path, my heart beats so fast that I fear I may suffer an attack. What is it with this holy man? Why can't I get him off my mind?"

She smiled and sat up in bed. She replayed the scene of earlier in the day in her mind. He had stood up for her when Tanko was onto her and his intervention had swept her off her feet.

There was a soft knock on the door. She beamed as she stared at the door. Her heart skipped at the realization that Yusuf would be at the door. She strengthened her ruffled dress and went to get the door.

"Nobody has ever beaten me at chess," Yusuf said.

Jumai smiled. "We'll see about that. Come on in." She opened the door wider.

Yusuf sat on the floor. Jumai got a pack of juice and two plastic cups before sitting next to him. They soon settled on an intense game of chess.

"Checkmate," Jumai said and threw a pillow at Yusuf.

Yusuf stared at Jumai and bit his lower lip to stop himself from kissing her. He wondered what her reaction would be if he took her hand in his and dropped soft kisses on her knuckles. His face turned sullen as his reality would not allow him to love this way. He was a walking corpse that was not entitled to an afterlife on this earth. He suddenly felt an urge to speak to her about who he was.

"I have something to tell you, but I'm afraid there is no time." His voice trembled.

She frowned. "You are burdened about something. I see it in your eyes."

He sighed. "Jumai, I won't lie to you. You have been a joy to me since I met you. I have never known this kind of happiness, more so from someone who is far above my class."

"All humans are equal, Yusuf."

Yusuf smiled weakly and rubbed his palms. "You honour me, Jumai."

"You are a man of honour, Yusuf. But tell me, what burdens you."

He took a deep breath and stared at his feet. "To put a light in my life, I had a romance with darkness. Now I regret the decision because my heart has found solace in your beautiful smiles. But with the heavy cloak of gloom around me, the feelings I've for you will definitely fade before it brightens."

Jumai shook her head. "Yusuf, you've got me all confused. What are you trying to tell me?"

Yusuf wriggled his hands. "My true mission here is to…"

"Yusuf." Inuwa banged on Jumai's room door.

Yusuf panted and looked at the door. Inuwa and Danladi burst into the room with condemning looks. How did they come in? How did they know that he was in Jumai's room? His heartbeat is fast as he continued to stare at Inuwa and Danladi.

"You. Traitor." Inuwa bellowed.

Yusuf paled. He got to his feet and grabbed Jumai to stand behind him. Inuwa pointed a gun at him with a deep scowl etched on his face.

"Blood for blood. From here on, there is no return." Inuwa shouted.

"Inuwa. Baba, please, no." Yusuf begged amidst Jumai's muffled cries.

"The penalty is death." Inuwa pulled the trigger.

Yusuf let out a piercing cry.

Yusuf cried out of sleep and jerked off the bed. He looked towards the door while trying to calm his breath. He looked at his wristwatch and realized that it was still noon. He looked at his side and he heaved a deep sigh of relief to see Jumai was sleeping peacefully. He caressed her beautiful face and pecked her forehead.

He rubbed his face with his palms. His dream was disturbing, and he would do anything to protect Jumai from any harm. His phone rang and he took the call without checking the name of the caller.

"Yusuf, where are you?" Garuba yelled over the phone.

Yusuf yawned and stretched an arm. "I'm around. What's happening?"

Garuba snickered. "Around where? I don't see you anywhere. Anyway, Inuwa is on his way here. So quickly get your ass over here."

Yusuf grumbled. "Thanks. I'm on my way."

He glanced at Jumai and caught sight of the chessboard lying beside her. They had slept off after playing the game several times. He rose to his feet quietly, tiptoed to the door. He looked back as Jumai yawned and scratched her eyes. He smiled and let himself out of the room with the hope that no one tries to get in after him.

Yusuf dragged his feet to the meeting place. Kawu met him halfway and clamped him on the shoulder. They walked towards Inuwa.

"Yusuf, where have you been? I just asked Kawu about you." Inuwa said without taking his eyes off Yusuf. He wondered what Yusuf had been up to away from the boys. He looked beyond Yusuf to see if no one was on his track. He was yet to trust Yusuf. He feared Yusuf would betray them one day. All the show of loyalty in the past months was not enough to convince him. His suspicion increased when he did not find Yusuf amongst his teammates on his arrival.

Yusuf braced his shoulder and cleared his throat. "I normally take a stroll. What is it?"

Inuwa smirked. "We have to leave now. The mission is going down earlier than expected. Baba Danladi sent me to get you all. Get ready, soldiers. We're pulling out in five minutes."

Yusuf's heart sank at the new information. He could not display his hurt over the new development, because it might land him in trouble. Any mood swing meant someone was about to falter or betray the brotherhood. He knew Inuwa was highly observant on that aspect. "But we have three days left for the cleansing."

"I know but an opportunity has emerged which we cannot ignore. We have to leave now." He signaled to Kawu and the other soldiers.

Yusuf sighed and nodded. He cast a forlorn look at Jumai's room window. He wished there was enough time to say goodbye.

He got into the car with the others and the driver pulled out of the compound swiftly to the direction where fate awaited him.

CHAPTER TWENTY-FOUR

The sun broke out slowly and played on Inuwa's dark countenance. He looked at his wrist and thought this was the perfect timing for another great disaster to rock the city. The vehicle sped down the highway at the speed the Danladians would love to carry out their next mission, unhindered and express delivery.

Inuwa glanced at Yusuf and spoke; "We were able to get some crucial information from one of our supporters. It was quite fortuitous. Allah is with us."

Yusuf nodded and turned to face Inuwa. "So, we have a confirmed target?"

Inuwa smiled. A deep frown creased his forehead. "Yes, the Apostolic Worship Centre. We've had one of our Libyan-trained specialists working on some explosives. It will be massive."

Yusuf sighed at the new fate that awaited him. "I am ready."

Inuwa smiled and patted him on the thigh.

They arrived at the camp by 8:00 am. Yusuf waited outside beneath a tree, staring at his new gun, while the others moved into the darkroom to meet Ishaq, the Libyan Specialist. He was busy at work with a headlamp attached to his forehead. If he was aware of their entrance, there was no trace anything could distract him from his work. Kawu and the others stood enthralled by his skillfulness. Ishaq smiled as he successfully connected a piece to the object he was building on a desk.

Ishaq concluded the decoration of the vest laden with explosives. He assisted Kawu in adorning the vest. Kawu put on a jacket over the vest while Ishaq stared at his new creation with satisfaction.

An hour later, the others assembled beside the mini-van to convey them to the venue. They took their seat and awaited Inuwa's instruction.

Inuwa walked up to them and gave a victorious smile. "Make sure you sit with the weapon at the scene and retain a smile as you embrace Allah." He said aloud. He gave Yusuf an intense stare. "Yusuf, you are to leave all your bullets inside the heart of the pastor. Make no mistakes."

Yusuf nodded.

Inuwa bade them farewell, and the vehicle zoomed off.

Jumai stirred from sleep. She woke up to see that it was already morning. She scanned the room in search of the one person that has captured her heart. She found the chessboard beside her. She wrapped her arms over her upper body. She had thought that she would wake up beside him.

The slight knock on the door broke her thoughts. She scrambled on her feet and moved towards the door. She opened the door to a maid who was bearing a tray of breakfast.

"Good morning, my lady." The maid bowed in greeting.

"Good morning."

"Master Maliki said I should bring you breakfast."

Jumai rubbed her sleepy eyes and flashed a grateful smile. "Thank you." She closed the door slightly.

The maid walked in and dropped the breakfast on the dining table by the corner of the room. Jumai yawned and opened the door wider for the maid to go out.

The maid stood by the door. "Do you need anything else, my lady?"

She wondered if Yusuf had had anything to eat. It would be nice and romantic to get him breakfast. "Yes. I need you to take breakfast to one of the holy men."

"Holy men?"

"Yes. Yusuf Ibrahim. That's his name."

"Oh, I'm sorry my lady. The holy men are gone. They

left this morning. All of them." She lowered her eyes.

"Left? To where?" She panicked.

The maid bowed. "I've no idea, my lady." She stepped into the corridor. "Enjoy your breakfast."

Jumai smiled weakly and closed the door.

The mini-van pulled to a halt beside the targeted huge building located at the centre of the city. There were clusters of people and vehicular movement about the perimeters.

Yusuf watched the passersby and motorists for a while before he shifted his gaze to the others who were already strapped in their white oversized attires while Ishaq rolled out instructions for the mission in a subdued tone. Yusuf did not dress up like the others. He had chosen to adorn corporate attire and a turban.

Ishaq clapped his hands softly. "We are here. Remember to flip the switch at the exact time as I have shown you. Allah shall be with you all."

"Allahu Akbar." Yusuf hailed.

"Allahu Akbar." The others replied in unison.

Kawu tapped Yusuf on the shoulder. "We meet in paradise."

Yusuf nodded and sighed as soon as the others alighted

from the van. He checked for his weapon, satisfied that it was there, he patted it one last time. Brief flashes of his last moment with Jumai played in his mind. He smiled fondly and became pensive when he heard the loud thud of his comrades hitting the ground in haste to accomplish their mission. Determination replaced the worried expression on his face as he bounded off the van. His eyes darted around the building. He nodded and walked into the building.

CHAPTER

TWENTY-FIVE

Maliki was writing on his desk in his small, air-conditioned office when Jumai walked in. Jumai's brisk entrance surprised him, and he quickly suspended writing. "My lady."

"Good morning, Maliki. I'll be leaving today."

"Ah. It's been nice having you around, Ma."

Jumai smiled. "It's been my pleasure."

"Please, extend my regards to your father. Please, do put in a good word for me as you can see, I'm running this office very well." He grinned.

Jumai smiled. She drew her veil tightly to shield her face. "I will. He should be on his way home."

She turned to leave but stopped. She turned to face him. "Please, I need to ask you some questions."

"What is it, my lady?" He looked concerned.

"It's about those holy men. Where did they come from?"

Jumai's question took him by surprise, and he stood. "You don't know?"

Jumai shook her head in firm denial and Maliki sighed deeply before taking his seat.

Pastor Joseph wondered if the message he was preaching touched the hearts of the people. He dabbed his face with a handkerchief. By the time he saw a few heads nod in response to his previous statement, he flashed a small smile. He signaled to one of the pastors to regulate the air-conditioner because he was starting to feel cold from the altar.

He continued preaching of heaven and hell, then the end of days soon to come. For some reason, he began to feel uncomfortable. A thought came to him to end the sermon and tell his multitude of keen listeners to go home. He shoved the thought aside and allowed his eyes to roam all the way to the crowd of worshippers seated at the balcony overlooking the altar.

Yusuf stood at the door of the Apostolic Worship Centre; the ushers seemed oblivious to his presence. Everyone seemed carried away by Pastor Joseph's teaching. Yusuf's eyes darted to the corner where he beheld Kawu's grim eyes. Kawu nodded at him and blinked his eyes.

Yusuf inhaled slowly and took out his weapon with

wobbly hands. He knew that this was the time to act bravely and impress those behind the cause, but it seemed his cloak of confidence had been ripped off.

Pastor Joseph's preaching became fiercer.

Yusuf began to creep forward. He discovered a good position just by the door and squatted. He glanced to the side to see if he was being trailed or keenly observed. He looked around and saw a CCTV directed to his position. He fixed his stare on the camera and Jumai's voice infiltrated his thought.

He heard her sonorous laugh, and the shape of her face took form in his mind. Yusuf shook his head and seemed to have forgotten about the CCTV. He saw Kawu at the other corner, muttering his last prayers, while Pastor Joseph continued to preach with a vibrancy to convert every worshipper present to righteousness.

Yusuf exhaled slowly and clutched the gun tightly to his chest. He remembered his most intense moment with Jumai. He remembered that while they were playing the game of chess, his daughter, Jumai had whispered *'stay with me.'*

Yusuf's eyes darted towards Kawu who was still praying. He turned to Pastor Joseph and broke into a sweat. There was no way he could do this.

'Since you don't have a phone, take my number. Call me when you lay your hands on a phone.' Jumai's voice floated to his ears.

Suddenly, the church went silent as a graveyard without mourners. The silence was deafening enough for him to hear his heartbeat wild. He clutched the gun tighter.

Kawu hollered suddenly, "Allahu Akbar." And the bomb exploded.

Yusuf recoiled slightly from the jarring blast. Almost immediately, there was another jarring sound outside. The auditorium vibrated. And the blast threw the centre into chaos.

Yusuf moved deftly towards the altar. He caught sight of Pastor Joseph crouching by the pulpit. Yusuf pointed his gun at him.

"Brother, please." Pastor Joseph's voice trembled.

Yusuf's voice quivered. He was on the verge of tears. "Forgive me, Pastor."

Yusuf pulled the trigger and fired two shots. He dropped the weapon and fled. The crowd scattered in pandemonium. Yusuf fought his way through the fleeing crowd towards the door.

Another round of blasts was heard, and more people screamed in fright.

Yusuf pulled off his turban and threw it away before he meandered into the crowd. Despite being absorbed into the crowd, he spared some glances to note if anyone was on his trail. His eyes were moist from the explosion's fog. He took a turn that led him to the rear of the building, and he saw Inuwa terminating three teammates.

It was shocking that Inuwa was here when he had not accompanied them on the mission. "Did he follow us without our knowledge?" He shook his head. "That's not possible." He was about to take a step back when Inuwa's phone rang, and he stopped from striking the next victim.

"Hello, Sir," Inuwa said in an impatient tone.

"Is the mission accomplished?" The caller's voice boomed from the speaker.

"Yes, Sir. Kawu and Yusuf embraced Allah swiftly but I'm sending three disobedient soldiers to Allah at the moment. I'll hang up now to call you when the job is done."

Inuwa ended the call and lowered his head to the soldier. "Blood for blood."

"Eye for an eye." The soldier responded.

"From this point."

"There's no going back." The soldier solemnly said and

bowed.

Inuwa shot him dead upon the last word.

A soldier caught Yusuf watching them. "Yusuf," he yelled.

Yusuf took to his heels and Inuwa turned swiftly and began to shoot at him.

A red saloon car squeaked and parked in front of Yusuf. Scared that it could be Inuwa or one of the soldiers, he bent to look and saw Ishaq behind the wheel.

"Get in Quick. Hurry," Ishaq gestured at Yusuf and opened the door from within.

Yusuf looked at the deserted road and thought he could not run farther on foot. He nodded at Ishaq and got into the car. Ishaq stepped on the accelerator and drove off at full speed.

"Why did you save me?" Yusuf asked after he was sure that they were miles away from the tragic scene.

Ishaq gave him a knowing smile. "Your lover asked me to." He focused on the road.

He frowned. "My who?"

He chuckled. "Jumai. Do you think we don't know your little secret? She said I should make sure you come back to her alive."

He shook his head. "She knows? How is that possible?"

"She's the only daughter of Alhaji Biu. Who happens to be our sponsor?"

Yusuf gasped. "You don't mean it."

Ishaq smiled slyly, "I kid you not."

They were now on a bushy path. Yusuf tapped his thigh softly as he awaited Ishaq's response to his question. He raised an eyebrow when it seemed it would take Ishaq an eternity to give him an answer.

Ishaq cleared his throat. "Yes, but the brotherhood has a different plan. We have grown beyond the bounds of politicians and their selfish needs. We have decided to focus on what we truly believe in."

Ishaq stepped on the accelerator for speed as he tried to evade the sweltering sun trickling into the car.

Yusuf's eyes were red from unshed tears. "I'm sorry, Jumai." He shook his head. "I should've told you." He whispered.

Ishaq glanced at him. "Why are you sad? Cheer up. The mission was not a success. Jumai will not be mad at you. Jumai has fixed no blame on you. She is not on her dad's side." He said happily.

"Does the Hotel belong to her father?" He stared at Ishaq in disbelief.

"Yes. She had to play nice so that no one would notice.

But then, she fell for you. She confided in me."

"So where are we going?" He kept his eyes on the bushy path.

"To meet Jumai." His mouth pressed into a cocky grin.

The car veered off the bushy terrain and suddenly, the car began to jerk. Ishaq stared at the steering wheel in the wonder of what must have gone wrong. The car finally stopped. He tried to start the ignition, but the car would not budge.

Yusuf was lost in thought, wondering what had gone wrong.

Ishaq turned to Yusuf. "Let me check the battery head." He opened the door.

"You think that's the problem?"

"It has to be. The bumpy road must have disengaged it."

Yusuf shrugged. "Have a look at it. And be fast about it, please."

Ishaq strolled to the front of the car and opened the bonnet.

After several minutes, Yusuf frowned. "Is everything okay?"

"Yes."

"Okay." He stopped frowning and relaxed into his seat.

Ishaq wiped off the sweat on his face and sat in the car.

He stealthily tried to reach for his gun in the compartment but found it empty. He frowned and frantically searched for it. His heart skipped when he felt something cold on his nape. The details of his gun were not lost on him. His eyes darkened as he slowly raised his hands above his head.

"Why?" Yusuf's lips trembled. He could hear his heartbeat rapidly.

"Because you're a bastard," Ishaq said with disgust.

Yusuf frowned. He gently got out of the car and dragged Ishaq through his seat. He put the gun on Ishaq's back and propelled him into the bush.

Ishaq snickered. "You're such an idiot. Your assignment was to simply kill that infidel with a pastor's tag, but no, you let him live. They have you on camera. Very soon they will apprehend you and you will ruin all our efforts. You will bring all our years of struggle to nothing."

"So, you lured me here to kill me."

"No, I brought you here to sing a love song." He gloated. "The brotherhood settled your family, we gave a new life to your daughter, yet your insatiable desires won't keep your balls in your loose jeans and concentrate on your primary assignment which is to simply die as you're told."

"So, Jumai doesn't know after all?"

Ishaq chuckled nervously. "Does this look like the

affairs of women? Only weak men like you yield to the sweet savor of a woman. She doesn't even know her father is our sponsor. Her father depends on the funds from international aides and the government. He gives us the guns and Allah guided us, we execute the missions."

"Oh, shut up. You have no fear of Allah. How can you smile at the pains of innocent people?"

"Oh, come on, Yusuf. Save these preaching for the mosque. You joined us at your free will. Were your senses dead? The truth is; we all do things we don't want sometimes. All humans are guilty of that crime." He replied nonchalantly.

He dug the gun into Ishaq's back and he gasped. "For the last time, does Jumai know about this?"

He turned slightly. "You should save the worries for your family, not Jumai. Inuwa is going to rape your little girl before slitting her throat."

Yusuf hit Ishaq's head with the gun and he fell to the ground. His heart pounded with fear. The thought of Inuwa raping his daughter tore at him. "Answer me." He bellowed.

"You're a dead man, Yusuf. You can't run away from us, we bought you, we own you." He pealed long throaty laughter.

Yusuf's face hardened as he pointed the gun at him. "Only Allah can say that. Journey well." He shot Ishaq in the heart. Yusuf took Ishaq's phone from his pocket and spat on the corpse.

CHAPTER TWENTY-SIX

Aisha barged into Ola's office looking pale. He stopped working on his laptop and glanced at her.

"There's been an attack at the Apostolic worship Centre."

Ola paled instantly. "What?"

"Pastor Joseph has been shot." She added.

Both bolted to the scene, they dashed through the blasted area. Ola shook his head as he ran past the once beautifully decorated building now turned into a dilapidated structure with a huge segment of the building still on fire. The duo meticulously investigated the incident with Aisha scribbling on her notepad. When they got to the spot where Yusuf shot Pastor Joseph, Ola squatted and glanced upward. He caught sight of the CCTV and nodded.

Ola played the CCTV and pause it when he spotted Yusuf. He looked to Aisha. "This man is not a killer. He's running from something." He frowned.

Ola's words left Aisha bemused. She failed to understand Ola's vindication of the man in the footage. That the man looked scared did not exonerate him from being a murderer.

"He had the chance to assassinate the victim, but he only made a mark. He's trying to tell us something." Ola grew pensive.

"What if he missed the hit?" Aisha wrapped her knuckles on the table in speculations.

"He can't miss at that close range."

They shared a knowing look.

Aisha did not understand what her colleague was trying to say. The man they had seen on the camera at the Apostolic Worship Centre was a killer as far as she was concerned. "And why do you believe that?" She sat on the chair facing him.

"Yusuf is one of those men whose families were paid wholesomely to execute suicide missions for the Danladians." He imagined himself in Yusuf's shoes and shook his head.

An officer opened the door and walked in. "Sir, we found the man, his name is Yusuf, he's from Gandi community. His father died a few months ago, he has his mother and a daughter. He's a graduate of Ile-Ife University."

The level of Yusuf's education stunned Aisha and Ola.

"Is he a graduate?" Aisha stuttered.

The officer continued. "From our investigations, Sir..."

"Wait." Ola stood from his seat and kept his eyes on Aisha.

"If Yusuf fails his mission, then only one thing is certain." He paused briefly in an attempt to unravel some puzzles.

Aisha nodded in agreement. "The Danladians will come for him, starting with his family."

"That kind of man would die to protect his family," Ola added.

"And that's why he joined the Danladians in the first place," Aisha said.

"Hurry, get the team together, get his image to every police station, every government agency, military, paramilitary, everyone," Ola shouted.

"Right away, Sir." The officer saluted and rushed out.

"The suspect is heading towards Gandi and we must get there before him. Move out." Ola rushed out of the office with Aisha running behind him.

It was midday when the knock on the door interrupted Jumai's thoughts. She had been staring out through the window since she last spoke to Maliki. She had taken her bath and changed into a comfortable silky gown as if that would soothe the questions that threatened her existence. She walked to the door and opened it.

The maid peered in and walked in half-excited. "My lady."

"What on earth is the matter?"

"There was an assassination attempt on Pastor Joseph at the Apostolic Worship Centre a few moments ago. By the Danladians, I'm sure." She exclaimed.

The information left a horrific expression on Jumai's face. "Wayo Allah." She touched her chest.

"They even have the face of the gunman on camera." The maid added.

Jumai's eyes widened. "They have the footage?" She shook her head and thought fast. If they had the face of the gunman on tape, she had to see it.

Jumai did not stop the tears that rolled down her cheeks. If tears could bring her Yusuf back, she would cry an ocean. If tears could erase the face of Yusuf from the tabloids, she would cry her eyes out.

She turned off the TV and continued to stare at the blank

screen. The image of Yusuf on the news mapped as a 'wanted person' flashed through her mind again.

"How could you do this to me? I love you." She said softly.

Her head throbbed and her heart ached. She could not stop crying and her eyes turned crimson.

CHAPTER TWENTY-SEVEN

Alhaji Suleiman glanced at Mairo and the driver. "This means that in three days, we will have lion faces at the primaries. On a political scale, he's losing ground due to the irrepressible state of insurgency in the country."

"You are correct, Alhaji." Mairo scrolled through his phone. He was reading the news on the Danladians' latest strike. He turned to Alhaji Suleiman and whispered. "Alhaji, is it possible that you may have a hand in the Danladians' executions?"

He looked at him with disdain. What exactly was wrong with Mairo? "What? Have you been smoking, Mairo?"

Mairo's hands shook. He suddenly wished that the car would stop so he could jump to evade Alhaji Suleiman's wrath. "I'm sorry, Alhaji. I've only asked one honest question."

"My interest is in the betterment of this country. We must speak out. Speak the truth irrespective of who might be involved. But how can you associate me with these terrorists? I was rudely interrogated because I volunteered to speak up for the interest of my people. And it does not mean I should bear the brunt of the president's incompetency and failure to nab the masterminds." He hissed. "Mairo, I never thought you could be so foolish."

✻ ✻ ✻

Jumai's phone vibrated incessantly. She weakly glanced at the screen and saw her mother's call. She tapped on the receive button and pressed the phone to her ear.

"Mom?" Her voice was hoarse from crying.

Simbi's frantic voice flooded the speaker. "Jumai, where are you? Are you okay? There was a bombing."

"I'm aware, mother. I'm coming home."

Simbi sniffed. "Okay. Be careful, my dear. The city is not safe."

Jumai nodded and ended the call before her mother could make more frightening comments She put the phone in her handbag and rubbed her face with a hand in exasperation.

CHAPTER TWENTY-EIGHT

Yusuf rested his back against a tree and panted. He was breathless after walking through the forest for hours. He looked around the forest in search of a path to lead him out of it. He needed to get to Gandi before Inuwa or the Danladians. He wondered if his family was safe.

Gunshots made him discard his thoughts and he quickly took cover behind the tree. He could hear sharp hollering from a distance, and he knew that he was in danger. He took off in a mad race. Five ruthless Danladians bounded after Yusuf.

Yusuf stopped running for a moment and fired some shots at his pursuers. He killed two men and resumed running. He hid behind a tree and killed another Danladian.

The other Danladians nodded urgently at each other. They disperse and began shooting at Yusuf and howled like demons from hell. More Danladians appeared from different angles of the forest.

Yusuf hid behind a huge tree and grimaced. He dropped to the floor and opened fire on the oncoming Danladians. He got to his feet and angrily advanced on them. He shot sporadically and smiled slyly when he saw some Danladians drop dead. He hid behind a tree again, panting.

Two more Danladians began to close in on him.

Yusuf could hear their footsteps. He held his breath, suddenly come in view, and shot them dead. He sighed and tossed aside his weapon. He stood to run away but felt a gun on his forehead. He slowly raised his eyes to his assailant. He smiled sadly and raised his hands.

"*Mayaki.*" Garuba shouted.

"We are just pawns, Garuba." His voice trembled. He was on the verge of tears.

"Perhaps, but you know how this works. We signed up for this."

"Yes. But it doesn't have to be that way, Garuba. I found a reason to live again. I found the purest of love." A faint image of Jumai floated across his mind. "Jumai, she changed everything for me. I want…"

He shook his head. "I'm sorry, Yusuf. There have been too many lives lost, too many oaths. Many promises have been committed into this."

"You can't put that on me, Garuba. I did what I had to

do to survive."

"You overstepped your boundary, Yusuf. Don't dream too much. Jumai is forbidden fruit." He yelled.

His voice was laden with emotion. "Love is not planned, my friend. Love just happens."

"Then you know that if I don't kill you, they'll kill me and my family."

"Garuba, please. If I must die, let it not be by your gun." He pleaded.

"I'm sorry, Yusuf." Garuba smiled weakly. "You and the brotherhood leave me no choice." He closed his eyes and inhaled deeply.

Yusuf closed his eyes and willed Garuba not to pull the trigger. He did not want to die by the gun of his best friend.

The chirping birds flew away at the sound of gunshots.

Shortly after combing the bushes for Yusuf, Inuwa was enraged that he escaped. Inuwa wiped his flaring nose as he scampered back to his seat with his smoking gun. The birds were singing different dirges. He looked from the dead soldier he had just shot to the others who were doing their best to hide the fear in their eyes and barked. "You're sorry? How sorry are you now?" He glared at them. "Now search everywhere. I want Yusuf dead or alive!"

The soldiers scurried off to avoid being the next to get

the attention of Inuwa's wrath. They rushed into their vans and drove off.

"We can do this, Garuba." Yusuf pleaded. His heart skipped. The other Danladians were getting closer now.

"Too late, Yusuf. Inuwa is already on his way to Gandi."

They heard a firing shot and Garuba dropped dead.

Seeing that his friend had been shot, Yusuf took to his heels. He ducked and ran a snake race to dodge the sporadic shootings on his trail.

Inuwa and his team zoomed past, and a police convoy followed their car.

Yusuf ran until he could see a tarred road. He found an empty van with no one in it; he looked sideways, satisfied that the owner was not in sight, he turned on the ignition of the car and stepped on the accelerator. He heard a man yelling by the bush path. He mumbled an apology and drove off to Gandi. He needed to save his family.

Inuwa and the Danladians continued in search of Yusuf. They ransacked every house along the lonely road.

Danladi parked his car on a safe side of the road. His anger was evident as he banged his head on the headrest.

✳ ✳ ✳

Jumai alighted from the car in tears and walked into the mansion.

"What is it, Jumai? Why are you crying?" Simbi rose from her seat. She had heard the sound of the car and it excited her to hear her daughter's familiar footsteps.

Jumai had not expected to see her mother in the living room. She avoided her mother's questions and walked past her. She desperately needed to be alone.

Jumai was still sobbing in her room when her phone beeped. She glanced at it and glimpsed a weird message. She opened it and read. *'The place where troubled hearts find succor. 3 PM.'*

CHAPTER TWENTY-NINE

Yusuf's mother and little Jumai scurried out of a provision kiosk. She was grateful for their little luxury. All thanks to Yusuf. She held Jumai's hand as they walked towards their hut. She glanced at her granddaughter. She was all she had now. Her face turned somber with guilt.

Yusuf parked at a distance and alighted from the van. He looked around in fear. He watched them approaching the hut and he came out of hiding and rushed to meet them. At that moment, the hut exploded, and Yusuf landed on the ground.

The Danladians opened fire on him. The police began to exit their hide-spots and began to shoot sporadically. Gunshots saturated everywhere and Yusuf escaped.

"Freeze," Aisha yelled. She had followed Yusuf the moment she caught sight of him.

Yusuf halted and took a step backward.

"Not one more step," she cocked her gun.

Ola rushed towards Aisha. "Get him," he commanded two officers.

The two officers handcuffed Yusuf who had tears streaming down his cheeks.

Yusuf wept silently and wished he could revoke the past. He gripped the prison bars tightly and hollered at an officer. "Officer," he beckoned on him to come close.

"What is it?" The male officer could not hide his disdain for the terrorist.

* * *

Inuwa led his team of Danladian soldiers into the police station and they began to shoot sporadically. He rushed into the cell corridor and found Yusuf hiding his face. He flashed a disdainful smile and broke into Yusuf's cell. He realized it was a dummy in Yusuf's clothes and he angrily shot at it. The police officer shook from beneath a bench in the cell.

Yusuf emerged from the back gates of the police station. He had managed to wear the police officer's attire. He began to run for his life not minding that tears blinded him now. All that mattered was saving his life and getting rid of the Danladians.

Inuwa pulled close to Danladi's car. He alighted from the car and joined Danladi in the back seat.

Danladi gave Inuwa a cold stare. "What is your problem? You have lost it. You took the boys for a mission without my permission, I told you not to confront the police. Yet, you attacked and even killed them. Now the government has tripled the manhunt for us by the inclusion of whistleblowers. The award is so attractive it can tempt our loyalists to rebel against us. I created this group for a purpose; I put you in charge for a purpose."

Inuwa took out a gun in a flash and shot Danladi and his driver. Danladi's blood splattered on the window. "I'm sorry I had to blow your brains out. You were ruining things for me." He spat on Danladi's shocked face and slid out of the car.

CHAPTER THIRTY

The sight of dead Danladians and wounded police officers rendered Ola and Aisha speechless.

"What happened here?" Ola directed his question to a frightened officer.

"The Danladians attacked us." The officer replied.

"And Yusuf?"

"He escaped."

Ola and Aisha hurried back to the car and zoomed off.

Posters of Yusuf were up on walls and handbills as a wanted person. Yusuf hid his face with a face cap as he walked by some desperate onlookers who wanted to turn in the criminal for a handsome reward. He saw a phone by a vendor's booth and snatched it. He tore into a mad race and the vendor began to shout, 'thief, thief, he stole my phone…'

✱ ✱ ✱

Jumai drew her veil tight as she moved with hasty steps oblivious of a stalker. She released her hold on the veil when she got to a dilapidated structure. She walked in and stopped, glanced at her wristwatch, and paced around in fear.

Yusuf emerged from behind, grabbed her with one hand, and closed the other hand over her mouth. "Hush."

She struggled and broke free, then slapped him across the face. "Get your bloody, filthy hands off me, you murderer."

His eyes became moist and his heart quivered. "Jumai listen, not everything you see on TV is true. Just let me explain for a minute." He pleaded.

"Oh really, Yusuf, you want to explain what part?" She scoffed. "That you're a terrorist who disguised himself as a holy man?" her voice broke. "Or the part that I foolishly fell in love with you without knowing a thing about you?" she sniffed. "You know what? My father works very hard to fight these terrorists. He's never at home, and I was busy falling for one of them. I was such a gullible woman."

"Jumai, please listen. I came back for you, and because I never had the chance to explain anything before our sudden mission. I was going to tell you everything."

She took a step backward.

"I joined the Danladians because, after the death of my father, the same illness affected my daughter."

"Wait, you have a daughter." She shook her head as a tear rolled down her cheek. She made to leave but he caught her hand.

"Jumai please…"

She shook his hand off her. "Leave me alone."

"She was going to die in 3 days. No one was willing to help. I gave my life in exchange for hers'. No father would want to sit and watch his child die. Please." He pleaded as though his life depended on it.

"What sense does it make if you have to kill others to protect your own from dying?" She barked. Another pain sliced through her heart. She felt betrayed.

"My Jumai's life was in danger." He watched her eyebrow quirk at his last statement and he knew that she was surprised. "Yes, her name was Jumai. She was beautiful, she had many dreams I just could not watch her die like that. But it doesn't matter anymore because." He burst into tears. "They're all dead now. The Danladians killed them because I could not kill Pastor Joseph."

Jumai weighed the options of running away and hugging Yusuf.

He fell to his knees sobbing. "You're the only one I have left."

She pulled him close for a hug. "I'm sorry."

"There's one more thing you need to know."

She pulled out of his arms. "What is it?"

"Your dad, he's not who you think he is."

"What are you talking about?" She frowned.

"Your dad is the sponsor of the Danladians."

She stepped away from him and her lips skewed in annoyance. "How dare you?"

He stood and took slow strides towards her. He did not stop until he was close to her that he could hear her panting. "Listen Jumai, it's top-secret. Your dad creates the chaos, and the government pays him to handle it. The world sees him as a peacemaker, but he is not. That is why we undergo purification at his guesthouse before our missions. We were deceived that we were working for Allah, and we have ten virgins waiting for us. They settle our families with cash rewards in exchange for our lives. Poverty has strangled many of my kind, so our lives were meaningless to us. They took advantage of our conditions and bought us over. We have…"

"Stop," she shook her head in disbelief. "I don't believe you and I don't ever want to see you again, here and the life after."

"Jumai, please, you have to believe me."

She ignored him and hobbled away with her heart struggling to reckon with these galling revelations.

Yusuf sighed and thought of his next move. He felt as though he was not alone. He turned around, a man punched him in the face, and he slipped into unconsciousness.

Three men dressed in black camouflages bundled him out of the uncompleted building.

CHAPTER THIRTY-ONE

"I hear you are the young man I have to thank for trying to ruin my dreams of becoming the President of this country. Thank you." Alhaji Biu crouched before Yusuf who had been roughly beaten and tied up in a sitting position.

Alhaji Biu observed the surrounding quietly and gave a derisive smile. He knew that no one would find them here. They were in one of his warehouses, far away from human habitation. "I heard they call you Mayaki, a fighter trained to die. Yet, you chose to live because of my daughter."

One of the soldiers punched Yusuf on the head.

Alhaji Biu glanced at him in disdain. He wondered why Yusuf was not dead yet. He remembered all he had done to get the boy killed. He had told Inuwa to get him killed because Yusuf was getting too close to his daughter. Inuwa had told him that Danladi had not given him orders. He gave a sly smile and vividly recalled the words he said to Inuwa.

"The rules are meant to be broken. Listen, it is time you boycott Danladi. He is becoming too weak. I will give you all the necessary support. She's my only daughter and I cannot afford to risk her in the hands of a condemned

man.”

He stared at Yusuf who spat blood. “Since all the means to kill you didn’t work. I guess your end will take place right here.” He gave a short laugh. “I told Kawu to ensure that you don’t come back alive in that mission. Danladi must be on his way to hell. Unfortunately, he did not do the will of Allah to get a deserving reward.” His voice turned cold.

Yusuf gasped in shock. “You killed him. He was my uncle.” One of the soldiers smacked him on the face and he coughed out blood.

Alhaji Biu gave a long throaty laugh. “Today, the party is going to pick me as the presidential candidate. I am going to stop all the bombings; I will be seen as the saint. Politics well played!” He grinned. He turned back to face Yusuf. The laughter suddenly disappeared. “Kill him!”

The guns of the Danladians clanged as they were cocked. They were about the pull the trigger and suddenly, a voice echoed.

“Don’t even think of it.” Jumai emerged from the darkest part of the warehouse.

Alhaji Biu froze in shock. The soldiers pointed their guns at Jumai.

She was aghast when she stood in front of her father.

"So, this is it, Baba?"

"What are you doing here?" Alhaji Biu barked in anger.

"What am I doing here? That is the best sentence you could pick to say to me. Baba, how could you? You are worse than the devil. So, you are truly behind the Danladians?"

The Danladians swooped in on Jumai with guns pointed at her head.

Horrified by their actions, Alhaji Biu yelled. "What are you doing? Get your guns off my daughter."

They withdrew from Jumai and let down their guns.

"How could you, Baba? Innocent women and children die from these bomb blasts. People have become homeless from these bomb explosions. How could you do this to your people?"

"Jumai listen, this is beyond your comprehension. Just get into my car I will explain everything to you." He pleaded.

"Go to hell, Baba. I owe it a duty to this nation to expose you and this devilish lot. I am disappointed in you. And listen, if a strand of Yusuf's hair goes missing, I will take my own life." Her stern face matched the finality in her tone.

Alhaji Biu yelled at his bodyguard. "Take her to the

car." He frowned and thought on how she came to know of his dark affairs.

Jumai struggled with the guard while Yusuf's heart lurched with pain as he struggled to set himself free so he could help Jumai. Just then, Alhaji's phone rang.

Alhaji Taminu's voice boomed on the phone's speaker. "Good news, Alhaji. We are sure of 90% votes for you today. Please, don't be late."

"Sure, I'm already on my way." Alhaji Biu gave a taut smile and ended the call.

"Alhaji," Inuwa said.

Alhaji Biu nodded. "I will handle it."

"Haba Alhaji, you know the rules. In case you have forgotten, it is blood for blood and eye for an eye."

Alhaji Biu swallowed and tried to hide his fear beneath a frown. "Do you realize you are talking about my only daughter?"

"I killed my only father, Alhaji. She must die."

"Now shut up and listen. I am an old man; if I were able, I would have had fifty children. I am now impotent. I know the rules, but all rules yield to exception."

"I cannot tell that to the boys, Alhaji" He glanced at the boys and raised an eyebrow to the affirmative.

Alhaji Biu sighed. "I will give you ₦20 Million, Inuwa."

Inuwa was thoughtful for some minutes. "Okay, Alhaji. But on one condition." He placed a finger on his lips. "She must keep her mouth shut."

Alhaji Biu nodded. "She will. I will make sure of that."

"I will kill Yusuf and put his head on a spike for our next news." He glared at Yusuf.

"Eh, Inuwa, you have to wait a little bit."

"Why Alhaji?"

"You heard Jumai. I cannot lose her and my reputation. I will release another ₦20 Million to you. Release him to me. I will find another means to kill him."

He glanced greedily at the other Danladians who were out of earshot and then he looked back at Alhaji. "Do it now."

He swiftly took his phone from his pocket and tapped on his bank application. There was a beep on his phone. "It is done. I have been debited. "Thank you. Thank you. I shall never forget this. I swear to Almighty Allah," he hurriedly rushed into his SUV and sped off.

Inuwa watched them go as the dust settled on his body.

CHAPTER THIRTY-TWO

Some minutes later, Alhaji Biu ordered his driver to stop the car and the escort vehicle abruptly halted behind them. He slid out of his SUV and ordered two guards to join the car conveying Yusuf and Jumai.

"Make sure he goes nowhere, today is my day. I must be present in that election."

"Okay, Sir." They chorused.

He got into the SUV and drove off, while the other cars took the left turn to their destination.

As soon as Alhaji Biu's car took the opposite direction, Inuwa sent his boys after them. Inuwa caught up with Alhaji Biu's escort vehicle and successfully kidnapped Yusuf and Jumai to an unknown location.

Yusuf stared at Jumai with so much love in his eyes. He felt bitter and helpless in this situation. Jumai winced as Inuwa menacingly walked towards her. Yusuf tried to free himself to shield her from any evil onslaught.

"This is the end of the road for you, Yusuf. First, I must go and show those politicians that I have grown beyond their reach and they must all die today. Nobody leaves that election venue alive." Inuwa squatted before Jumai.

"Today, I'm going to kill your father, my sponsor. It's called a boycott." Inuwa winked.

"And I pray your death finds you soon," Jumai spat in his face.

He slapped her cheek. "When I return, I will rape you mercilessly," He spoke in Hausa. His eyes roamed over her body lustfully. "While I let your Romeo view the fun." He laughed and walked away.

Inuwa pointed at two Danladian soldiers. "Keep your eyes on them." He and the other soldiers jumped into their vans and sped off.

Yusuf sadly stared at Jumai. "I'm sorry I involved you in all these. I did not know one's soul could be attached to the other until I met you. You restored the peace I never had."

"Stop talking, Yusuf. It's too late for love sermons now." She whispered.

"I'm sorry."

A soldier with a large scar at the side of his face lit a cigarette. The other soldier tried to molest Jumai, while Yusuf struggled helplessly. Just then, some strange footsteps caught their attention. The smoker threw his cigarette and stepped on it.

Tanko walked towards them with a pistol and a sadistic

smile.

Yusuf's face turned sullen while Jumai's face was ashen with fear.

"Holy man." He crouched before Yusuf. "You're not so Jackie Chan anymore?" He chuckled.

"Are you part of this?" Jumai shook her head and hoped that before she dies, she would not have beheld any more surprises that would break her heart.

"Any man worthy to be called a man is part of this. I used the bodyguard services of the Danladians now and then. There is nothing more assuring than being protected by men who are sworn to death."

She sneered, "You bastard."

He smiled and rose to his feet. "Of course, I am an evil bastard. Now, I'm going to execute this idiot for the insult I suffered." He took a gun from his back pocket and pointed it at Yusuf.

"Tanko, don't," Jumai's voice trembled on the verge of tears.

Yusuf sighed with pain. "Thank you for the joy, Jumai. It was brief but it was the best time in my life. A light in my darkness and for that, I shall ever be grateful."

Jumai turned her head to Yusuf. She wanted to hold him in her arms, to tell him that it was not his fault. She wanted to tell him that her heart would still pant after him even in death.

Tanko flashed a cruel smile. "You are a fool."

Tanko's finger moved towards the trigger, Jumai could hear her pulse quicken to a tempo. In the realization that this was the end of the road for him, Yusuf bowed his head in prayers.

Inuwa's vehicle had not driven far off when he intuitively barked, "Stop the car." The Danladian's van stopped abruptly, and the driver put the gear in reverse.

CHAPTER THIRTY-THREE

Alhaji Biu could see other dignitaries troop in and out of the party headquarters. He alighted from the car and sighted Alhaji Taminu. Both men wore the same blue coloured kaftan they had deliberately picked for the day. According to Alhaji Taminu, blue was the colour of the sky and for them, the colour was like a good luck charm because; the sky was their starting point.

Alhaji Taminu spread his arms in a concerned gesture. "What happened? Why are you late?"

"My friend, for some minutes, my heart and an entire dream was in turmoil." He sighed.

"Do you mean it? Do you mind telling me about the experience?"

Alhaji Biu shook his head. He was clearly in no mood to answer such a question. They walked into the room where the party members and the delegates sat.

The Chairman mounted the podium to speak, "Distinguish members of this great party. It is of great delight that I bring to your notice the aspiring candidates for our next year's presidential election. Without further strain to your curious ears, I diligently inform you that Alhaji Suleiman could not make it here because of his involvements with terrorism."

Yusuf had heard gunshots and had waited to feel blood drip from his heart or for his lung to struggle for breath. He inquisitively opened his eyes and the sight of the dead Danladians surprised him. He reared in shock when his gaze met Tanko's. Tanko tug and cut at the ropes that bound Jumai. Yusuf flexed his body and realized he was already free.

"Quick. We need to leave here fast." Tanko's voice quivered.

"Tanko, why are you doing this? I don't know if I should thank you or wait for the worse." Yusuf said.

He should have killed Yusuf, but he did not know why he was helping them. Perhaps he loved Jumai and would do anything for her. He shook his head, "Now is not the time to think about love." He said softly. He untied Jumai and then picked up his pistol from the floor.

Inuwa got to the warehouse in time to see them running into the bush. He ordered his boys to open fire on them. Ola and his team arrived and began to open fire on the Danladians. Tanko fired at any man that wanted him dead, while the Danladians sporadically shot at the police.

The Danladian soldiers died from the gunshots of either the police or Tanko. Inuwa took cover. A bullet hit Tanko, and he fell to the horror of Jumai.

Jumai and Yusuf tried to resuscitate Tanko amidst the crossfire. Pain coursed through Tanko and he could see his life slipping away. He turned to Yusuf when he could not bear to see Jumai in tears. "If you hurt her, I will return from the dead and kill you." He whispered.

Jumai wept. "Tanko, please don't die."

Tanko turned to Jumai, raised his shaky hand slowly, and caressed her face. He wanted to tell her how much he loved her, but he breathed his last.

Jumai cried hard as she threw herself on Tanko's body. Yusuf got furious, picked up Tanko's gun, and began to gun down the Danladians on target.

Inuwa glanced at the remaining soldiers in rage. "Kill them all." He called two soldiers to his side and they slid into a van. "Those politicians must pay." Fury marked Inuwa's face as they drove off.

As soon as they left, the crossfire gradually died down with all the Danladian soldiers dead. Ola and Aisha ran towards Yusuf and Jumai.

"Why are you late?" Yusuf queried.

"We had some delay," Ola sighed while scanning the area. "Hurry up, we have to go."

The hall was thrown into a jubilant mood the moment the national chairman announced the voting result. Alhaji Biu could not stop grinning despite his cheeks hurting from the excitement. He had won the party's primary election.

"I want to thank you all for believing in me. I promise the party will not regret this decision. With this victory in my favour, winning the presidential election would be an easy feat." He bellowed into the mic.

The party members broke into songs of joy.

Inuwa drove into the premises and the car ground into a screeching halt. Ola and Aisha were not far from their wheels. The police officers were quick enough to arrest Inuwa and the other Danladians.

Ola and his team barged into the election's venue. Ola marched forward, "Alhaji Biu, you are under arrest for treason, felony, genocide, and terrorism." His heart skipped in excitement. He could not believe that they were finally apprehending the sponsors of insurgency in the country.

Alhaji Biu frowned. "You must be mad. I am the next president of this country. You don't have any evidence."

Ola shook his head. "Don't make it hard, Alhaji. We have plenty of evidence."

Yusuf emerged and shoved a chip into Ola's hand.

"Alhaji, we have evidence that will make you pay for all your crimes." Ola waved the chip at Alhaji. "We planted this chip in Yusuf. So, he can help us with a thorough investigation." He glanced at Aisha and smiled.

Alhaji gasped while some of the party members screamed in shock.

Alhaji Suleiman walked up to him. "It's funny how the cookie crumbles; you are not the smart and good guy after all." He sneered.

The police apprehended Alhaji Biu, and they left the building for the car park. A car pulled up in front of Yusuf, and the others. Little Jumai and Yusuf's mother alighted from the car. Yusuf screamed in amazement. He had thought that they had died from the explosion. He turned to Ola for an explanation.

Ola smiled softly. "We quickly pulled them out of the hut through the back door before the explosion."

A tear rolled down Yusuf's face. He mumbled, "thank

you." Little Jumai ran to hug her father.

Inuwa glanced at the pistol behind Ola's pocket. The sight of Yusuf hugging his family infuriated him. He gritted his teeth when Yusuf gave Jumai a warm reassuring smile and hugged her. This beautiful reunion was unbearable for Inuwa. He wished he had died so he could compulsorily go to meet his virgins. He glanced back at the gun and tried to snatch it from Ola.

Aisha sighted him in time and shot him. Inuwa dropped to his knees and fell to the ground.

In this instant, the million-selling action and political thriller with several twists are delivered… Brace yourself up for a bumpy ride!

Yusuf, a poor terrorist on his route to suicide mission finds Jumai, a daughter of Alhaji Biu, a brutal politician involved in creating mayhem in the country through terrorism. When the president who trusts him gives him money to fight terrorism, he uses it to enrich himself, his family, and weird power.

Biu's sponsorship of the sect is hidden even from his wife and only child until he discovers the relationship and Yusuf refuses to go for the mission. Now, he must swiftly use all at his disposal to stop the relationship, lest it jeopardize his presidential ambition of which he has won the primaries of the ruling party.

The whole world on the quest to know the faces behind the mask of terrorism is about to know who is behind the deadliest sect as the love bird threatens to expose all the politicians involved in sponsoring terrorism in the country if they do not allow him to marry the queen.

Yusuf is wanted dead or alive and the cat tears the bag, its haven.

Do you think they married?

About the Author

Chinazom Akobundu Godwin, was born in Imo State, Nigeria. He attended the Federal Polytechnic, Nekede, Owerri Nigeria, the Hartlepool College of Further Education, England, and the University of Port Harcourt, Nigeria.

He is a novelist, scriptwriter, and movie producer. **Boycott** is his ninth novel, and he has several unpublished manuscripts to his name.

He is happily married to Ugochi Blessing Godwin and their marriage is blessed with three children. He lives with his family in Bonny Island, Rivers State, Nigeria.

Author's Connect:

Win his next novel and have it shipped to your location by connecting him with fifty friends of yours.

How does it work?

Sign up or Follow him first on all his social media handles below, then send him private messages of the names of your friends before they follow him.

Let's have a chat with him about his books and movies.

Website: www.chinazomgodwin.org

Facebook Page: Chinazom Akobundu Godwin Books and Movies.

Instagram: chinazomakobundu

Twitter: @chinazomagu

Goodreads: Chinazom Akobundu Godwin